GODS OF THE BLACK GATE

THE SECOND BOOK OF THRICE DEAD

JOSEPH SALE

TWC
THE WRITING COLLECTIVE

In This Series

'The truth is darkness, and the only thing that matters is making a statement before one enters it. Cutting the skin of the world and leaving a scar. That's all history is, after all: scar tissue.'

— STEPHEN KING, *MR MERCEDES*

'You are a spirit, I know. Where did you die?'

— WILLIAM SHAKESPEARE, *KING LEAR*

To Kelly Pearson, for years of dedicated reading, and for saying she couldn't wait for this book.

To the dark gods, for they preside over us all.

THE SECOND READING

Y ou're still here? Well, that's good. A lot of people start running when they see what the cards have to show them. But even in the deepest darkness, there is light, no?

First, there was The Fool. Now, let's see what your second card is.

Ah, The Devil. That's one of the Big Three. Three cards that terrify the living daylights out of anyone who is having a reading: The Tower, The Devil, and of course Death. But don't be scared. Everything exists for a reason, even The Devil.

Take a long look at the card. See how the shackles bind the figures of Adam and Eve. These shackles represent our addictions, our vices, our bad habits. I can tell you have a few. And so do I.

But if you look at their collars more closely, they are large enough that our couple might take off the shackles themselves. It is within their power to slip the addiction. They are allowing themselves to be controlled by The Devil, to give in to his power to obsess those who look at him too long.

I don't blame them. The Devil can be very persuasive. He used to be the Lord of Light after all... When he speaks, it's with a serpent's tongue, a tongue that can whisper secrets and offer tastes of another universe.

I saw you flinch there. You still don't believe in other universes? You have glimpsed a few already via The Fool. You are about to glimpse another.

And this one belongs to The Devil...

Day -

23RD DECEMBER 2060

The coma was supposedly too deep for thought or dreams, but there was no darkness deep enough to submerge him.

Time was suspended here. Sense of place, too, had gone. There was only the black canvas and the fog-thick imagery which assaulted it, like an insect cloud rising from a fissure located somewhere in the shade of his mind. Places and people he had imagined and seen were visible in the cloud, perpetually fluctuating, as though his consciousness sought the correct tuning for an old TV.

At times the insects hummed into the shape of his father, creating a flowing silhouette of brown and yellow bodies. He knew it was his father because of the strange stooped gait and the too-many-teeth grin; his canines were formed from the abdomen of wasps.

The buzzing of insect wings reminded the sleeper of the time his father had once taken him into the place he worked: a corporate entity. His father was a salesman. The sleeper remembered the endless computer screens, the whine of the workmen, the desperate ring of the videographic calling technology: all of it amalgamated into a sound like a hornet's angry growl.

'Son!' A ripple of silvery wings. 'Son!'

The sleeper wanted to wake from this. He didn't want to speak with his father, or rather, the shadow of his father; too many years and disappointments had passed.

The thought of freeing himself from the artificial sleep spun in his head like a blazing Catherine wheel, never finding closure, leaving imprints on the dark as ephemeral as desert mirages.

Wake up! Wake up!

As though will alone could achieve it. The paralysing drug throbbed in his veins like the aftermath of alcohol. Nothing responded to his commands. If he could have smiled, he would have, despite it all: such measures showed just how afraid of him they were.

Do not gloat!

A painful stab of thought, like lancing a boil. The image of his father quivered but did not dispel. Rather, the command seemed to have come *from* him.

'You were a drone, da. Never anything but a drone. You thought you were conquering the world. But it had conquered you.'

You were the one who failed.

The words, formed from buzzing and rage, pierced deeper than the toxins in his bloodstream.

None of this would have happened if the sleeper had not failed in his mission. He had been given a purpose, a holy purpose, and he had not been able to execute it. What had gone wrong? Had the offerings been insufficient?

How was it someone could be so sure of something one moment and unsure of everything the next?

The world had him now. Like a mindless fly he was stuck to the glistening strands of its web. Soon the mechanical spider of the Law would mummify him and put him away in some secret, hidden place, never to see the light of day again.

The darkest hellhole on Mars.

He had no doubt that was where they were taking him. He could picture where he lay now: some table in a Government Carrier, bound and drugged so that he didn't interfere with the transport flight.

What hope could be salvaged from this?

None. It is over. It would be better never to wake.

But what fate was that? Trapped with the echo of his father forever.

Even as the despair caused the muscles in his chest to tighten, flickering briefly against their invisible restraints, the hornet-created image of his father disbanded and a new image surfaced.

The blackness peeled away to reveal a valley of ghostly bone: the eye-sockets of countless skulls shining like a thousand anti-matter portals. The whiteness of the bone shone with hateful light implying a watchtower activated and sleeping giants woken. He felt, suddenly, terror and exhilaration mixed like unstable alchemy. This was more than dreaming. A vision was being shown to him.

His purpose rekindled like an altar candle lit within a faithless ruin.

This was all part of *their* plan!

As soon as the revelation had occurred to him, the white bone of the skulls began to die, leaving only spots of final blackness on a shallower dark; each spot the cyclopean eye of a wormlike thing. Eyes that would never shut, could never be quelled, would outlast the stars.

The Gods still lived.

They were calling him.

Day 120

Caleb Rogers pulled out his earpiece, slipped it into the inner pocket of his jacket and rubbed his eyes. He swept a hand across the pale glowing monitor; it flashed once and blinked off. He didn't know how many times he'd listened to the interview or read the transcript in the one-hundred and fifteen days he'd been aboard the GC but every time he did he felt a little closer to understanding his adversary. Of course, he doubted anyone could ever truly understand a man like Craig Smiley, but he had to get some idea if he wanted to have any chance of finding him.

Just over three and a half months ago Caleb had been sitting at his desk drinking black coffee and talking out a case with his partner Tom when the Chief of Police had strode on up to his desk and said two words.

'Office. Now.'

Caleb had known Justin Walker long enough to realise as soon as he met his eyes that something had gone deeply wrong and that it wasn't something any other person in the room could handle. It was meant for him. It was personal. He and Tom stood, Caleb finished his coffee, and they followed Justin like kids pulled out of class by the headmaster until the Chief shut the emblazoned door to his office behind them and motioned for them to sit. They sat.

'What's this about?'

'Smiley.'

That one word was all Caleb had needed to feel his pulse quicken and his throat and mouth dry up as though someone stuffed a towel down his gullet.

'We put him away seven years ago.'

'There's been a problem on Mars.'

What followed was possibly the most painful thing Caleb had ever had to hear. Christ, he hadn't found it this hard when his dad told him his mother was gone.

'That's it, kiddo.' A small shrug. All his father could offer him.

A sixteen year old boy's world turned upside down with three words.

This was worse than that. He remembered odd details of the whole thing – like fragments from a dream: the stink of the leather chairs which smelled of the sweat of all the nervous fuckers that'd sat opposite Chief Justin Walker either pleading for their jobs back or silently bracing for the hurricane about to come out of his mouth. As Justin explained what'd happened, a vein twitched in his neck and his skin turned the colour of cherries. He spoke as though what'd happened on another planet two-hundred and twenty five million kilometres from Earth was somehow the failure of his department. Caleb just sat in silence and swallowed it like a draft of bitter poison.

'All transport to and from Mars has been grounded until we find him. The miners won't be happy but Command is not having him slip aboard a junker and get back to earth.' Justin sat back in his armchair as though exhausted. His skin turned blotchy as the colour drained out of him.

'So what's the plan boss?' Tom said.

'They've got their own internals on it, but the fact remains: we're going to have to send you guys out there too.' Justin ran his hand over his face so that red crescent-moons appeared under his eyes. Tom huffed. Caleb didn't say anything. He doubted anyone could have stopped him going out there whatever the line from Command was. He'd put Smiley away seven years ago and he would put him away again a hundred times if he had to. He'd never forget what he did to the girl in Houston. A picture said a thousand words, or so the motto ran. He wasn't sure about that, but what he was sure of is that it'd reached inside and touched his soul, changing who he was forever.

'It's over three months to get to Mars, boss,' Tom said. 'That's a third of a year. We've got new cases to run. It was bad enough taking him out there in the first place.' He looked to Caleb for support but he didn't meet Tom's eye. He was thinking real hard about what Smiley was doing right now as they sat in an office blustering.

'Your cases will be distributed amongst the others. Your flight leaves in two days.' Justin raised his hands in an *I can't help you* gesture and slapped them down on the table. 'Sorry Tom but it's just the way it is. You two worked on his case for a year. You're the best suited at finding him. I've notified Facility Six of your expected ETA.'

Justin let out a sigh, clasped his hands over his head and massaged his scalp.

'I know you've got a family Tom but we just have to get this thing under wraps.'

'You mean we have to be seen to be doing something.' Tom slumped back in his chair and blew the strand of flaxen hair that'd fallen over his eye, curiously adolescent. 'By the time we get out there he'll either be dead or they'll have found him. I mean think about it for a second. It's not as if he's got anywhere to go, unless they terraformed Mars since I last was there and forgot to mention it on the news. Even if he stole an oxygen suit he'd run out of air crossing the desert or just get arrested at the next mining colony he stumbled into.'

'I know, Tom. I know.' Justin said. The colour crept back up his neck like a hot liquid filling him up.

'I personally don't wanna have to take the chance with him,' Caleb said. He reached inside his jacket and pulled out a tobacco pouch, filter and cigarette paper and began to roll himself a light, holding the filter in his mouth like a mint. His fingers trembled slightly. 'I've put away plenty of crazies in my time but never anyone as smart-crazy as him. He's like you or me. He believes in what he's doing. And because of that he'll find any way he can to survive and get off that rock. And then if he can he'll come for the people that put him away.' He looked up. 'That's you Tom. And me.'

He finished rolling the cigarette and stood.

'We'll be on that flight Chief.'

And here he was now.

One-hundred and fifteen days of routine. Caleb Rogers was not someone who enjoyed repetition. Every day at 5:00 on the earth-time clock of the GC he woke to an alarm, undid the restraints that held him securely to his designated bed and donned his magnetic boots that would allow him to move through the ship's corridors with the illusion of gravity. He'd make his way to the gymnasium area and work-out for an hour. The work-out mostly consisted of lifting or running with magnetic weights of varying strengths to simulate the act of lifting a weight against gravity on earth. Caleb Rogers was also not someone who enjoyed fitness regimes, but it was a requirement of space travel and he could see the point. Without gravity the body deteriorated. He thought it something of a metaphor – people with nothing to struggle against got weak, soft. He wondered whether that was why Tom had gotten flaky ever since things started going well for him.

The first astronauts who'd manned the International Space Station had been out there for five years. When they returned to Earth everyone thought space slowed the aging process. The astronauts looked the same as they had when they'd left – eerily youthful, lacking the marks of strain so common among those confined to Earth that they'd become invisible.

After a few weeks, however, it became apparent their skeletal strength and muscular structures had been irreparably damaged; they were barely able to support their own weight now they'd acquired it again. Since then an official training regime had been established to prevent the deterioration. A lighter version of the regime was also required for the lower gravity inhabitants of Mars.

From the workout he then grabbed a coffee he had to sip through a straw and ate a meal of liquefied fruit, vegetable and protein that he also had to sip through a straw. He'd then replace his nicotine patch and chew gum like it was the face of his worst enemy.

For the rest of the day he worked. He played and replayed the interviews with Craig Smiley, looked over the old case files, delved and delved. There had always been something about the case, about the man, something that'd driven Caleb insane and yet driven him on. Maybe it was the brutality of the murders or maybe it was the artistry behind them.

Artistry? Some would say he was sick for using that word, but it was the only word Caleb had for what Craig Smiley had done. He'd made corpses into art. No wonder the Lone Star state had got scared shitless.

Tom Marvin said Caleb was obsessive and compulsive; he never denied it. Even after he'd gotten Craig Smiley and been assured he was being shipped off to the most secure prison facility ever built, not least of all because of its planetary locale, he hadn't been able to get the killer out of his mind. Or the girl. Some nights she still spoke to Caleb out of the yawning dark and he woke startled. Caleb didn't believe in an eye for an eye or a tooth for a tooth but he did wish he could change the law that'd passed in 2023 banning capital punishment and made an exception for Smiley. He was like a rabid dog: the only way to be sure it can't kill again is to put it down. Caleb had come toe to toe with enough psychopaths to know it was true.

'How many times you gunna listen to that shit before you realise the simple truth?'

Tom sidled into view in the doorway to his room, moving with the awkward gate the magnetic boots forced. He'd spent most of the trip calling his wife Melinda or helping himself to the ample supplies of whiskey he'd wangled into storage. Alcohol was not allowed on space-transports of any kind whether junker, Government Class or explorative, but Tom could be charismatic and persuasive when he wanted to be. He was the kind of man who could get even the glibbest tell-tale to keep mum by tapping his nose.

'What's that?'

'He's nuts.' Tom grinned, showing a horse's white teeth.

Caleb forced a smile.

As they stood swaying slightly with the motion of the deck Caleb thought, and not for the first time, about just how different they were. Tom Marvin was tall, oval faced and pale as his whitish hair. He wore a leather jacket and jeans, some old fashion from fifty years ago which was at odds with the clunky zero-g magnetic boots. He looked like a university student; there was something eternally scruffy about him. Maybe it was the lopsided way he smiled or his arms-folded stance, but he always stood like he was making conversation at a work party.

Caleb Rogers was a very different story. Rake-thin, dressed smart in a black shirt, suit trousers and a vintage jacket even older than Tom's leather one. It was his habit of wearing all black that led to the other detectives calling him the Funeral Man. His hair was short, military, black as well. Unlike Tom's thinness which suggested a lean diet and regular downtime on the tennis court, Caleb's thinness was a thinness of sleepless nights and haunting intensity, as though he was burning up from a fever that would always be with him.

'What's up?' Tom pressed.

'It's that line towards the end about him being "grateful" to be locked away on Mars I can't get over. It seemed like he was talking about something else, not just the Nemontemi.'

'Well shit,' Tom said, pacing around the room. Sitting wasn't comfortable or required until the ship came into atmosphere in which case they would strap themselves down to make sure nothing went wrong just before gravity kicked in. 'You're starting to sound like him. Good job we're almost there. Few more days of this and you'll start talking about star gods and offerings.'

Caleb gritted his teeth and nodded. He'd long given up snapping at Tom for not taking things more seriously.

Tom must have caught his look.

'Look, Cal, I did that interview and I'm telling you I didn't read anything other than he believed every word of the shit coming out of his mouth. You heard him and you said it yourself back in Justin's office. The Nemon-what's-it is real to him.'

That was true enough. Caleb had interviewed Craig numerous times. When he looked into most criminal's eyes, especially once they'd been caught and were facing sentence, he saw doubt. There was not a shred in Smiley.

'But he's escaped. It's a maximum security prison, Tom. On fucking Mars. He must have had something up his sleeve.'

Tom shrugged.

'Maybe. We'll find out soon, won't we?'

'True enough.'

A female voice crackled on the ship-wide intercom.

'Will passengers please move to the seating area and fasten themselves securely into the seats. We will shortly be entering atmosphere.'

Tom smiled.

'Right on cue.'

'Fuck me sideways.'

'You'll be fine,' Tom said, with his usual wink.

Caleb knew landing on Mars was no longer the feat it'd once been, but it still gave him the shakes.

When the first colonisers had been shipped to Mars - fifty or so volunteers either with little family left or family they'd rather have less to do with - there had been a world watching them with bated breath, anticipating every disaster imaginable. Automatic reconnaissance and research machines like Rover and Curiosity, and later the construction bots like Foundation and Builder, had successfully landed but they were machines and had no vital requirements. Transporting people was another thing altogether and it'd been thirty years in preparation. When at last they watched as the three pronged landing gear deployed and the ship glided to a safe landing, the sound of cheering could be heard from almost every homestead in Austin.

Now, it was supposedly just routine.

Caleb followed Tom to the seating area and buckled himself into his seat. It was a large square room with chairs set into the walls so that all the passengers would face inwards towards the centre of the room. All of the seats save two were empty. Caleb wondered whether the expense of shipping out two detectives was all part of making Justin's gesture of action to Command even grander.

He undid the button of his inner pocket, took out his packet of gum, flicked it open, popped one in his mouth and began chewing. He closed his eyes and replaced the packet. The ship began to vibrate and rattle as they entered the gravitational pull of the red planet. He told himself it was no different to a plane setting down. Caleb was the kind of man who had enough problems trusting someone else to drive his car let alone land him on a foreign planet. He wished there was a viewing window so he could see exactly what was going on rather than imagining the steady-handedness of the pilots giving out.

'I can't believe it.' Tom laughed, raising his voice slightly over the sound of rattling metal. 'The great Caleb Rogers defeated by flying.'

'If you ain't scared of space travel you ain't got brains,' Caleb growled.

'I'm hardly scared of anything,' Tom quipped. 'Not after the shit-holes we've been in, Caleb.' He winked and laughed. 'Dying from a crash ain't half bad next to getting gelded or skull-fucked to death. What do you reckon's the worst place you've ever been in?'

Caleb thought those words marked another critical difference between him and Detective Marvin: Tom was hooked on the thrill. However much he bellyached about being far from Melinda there was no getting round the fact he came alive as soon as there was a whisper of danger.

At least he was in the right profession.

The ship juddered and bounced as if in a current. Caleb had been told there were winds on Mars but without an ozone layer he struggled to understand how that was quite possible.

'You'd be surprised,' he said.

'Yeah?'

'It was in England: place called Boscombe. Went there on leave last year as I heard it had a nice beach and I've never been one for learning another language. The beach was decent but I could have done without the rest. Some kid got his head sawed off right in front of the police station there. Owed someone some money. Something like a few hundred bucks. Then there're heroin deals going down in broad daylight in the city centre. No one who can do anything about it gives a shit. I think that's the worst thing about it: it's not one of the estates you get in Texas where everyone and their mom is packing or doing coke. There're civilians living in the middle of the shit.'

'Jesus.'

'Yeah I'll take Texas any fucking day.' Caleb grinned despite himself. 'What's yours?'

'Honestly?' Tom said. 'Ain't nothing compares to that biker den we busted.'

Caleb laughed. That'd been in the early years of their investigations. He wasn't surprised Tom had picked it given that he'd blown his cover and almost been flayed alive. Caleb had gotten him out of that fix. Caleb got him out of a lot of fixes.

The ship pitched right and then dropped as if ducking gunfire. Caleb's laugh cut short and he gripped the armrests like they were the last handhold on a sheer cliff-face. His breathing grew shallow. Nausea mounted in his belly, a toxic fluid in his bowels overflowing to fill up his intestines and stomach. When he looked down at his right hand his wedding ring had cut off the circulation to his fourth finger.

Slowly, the craft stopped trembling and Caleb sensed they had entered a measured vertical descent, which meant the blast doors had closed over their heads and they'd reached the landing dock safely. Before he could breathe a sigh of relief, heaviness dropped over him like a mantle and left him a little giddy. He slid his feet out of the magnetic boots and wriggled his toes in the air. Gravity on Mars was at roughly 38% of Earth gravity and so he felt as light as a child, though he had enough weigh so that he no longer needed the belt to hold him down.

'You're getting better,' Tom said. 'You didn't look green this time.'

Caleb grunted.

<>ACCESS LOGS</>
  <>MARS CONTAINMENT FACILITY 006</>
  <>RECORD NO. 101007</>
  <>CREATED 10:42:55 27/12/2060 EARTH TIME</>
  <>BEGIN RECORD</>

So, Detective Rogers this time, is it?

Are you the good cop or the bad one? I must say I've heard a lot about you. I expect you're the good cop. Solving all the cases but getting none of the glory? But the real question is: are you going to *play* the good cop? Because you can choose to play just about anybody you like. We can all choose. It's a gift people don't even realise they have.

What role am I playing?

I would have thought it obvious? Then again, maybe it isn't so obvious to you. I'm the hierophant. Or perhaps a more modest term would be the good priest. And yes, I did what I did in the name of god.

Not your god, of course. The one who supposedly died on the silver thing around your neck. No. The seven true gods.

Names Detective Rogers? They do not have names. They simply are. Surely a man of your intelligence can see that beings which came into existence before even the formation of our solar system cannot have a name? They are like poems, Detective Rogers. And they are also the source of all poetry. Do you read poetry? I didn't think so. You share something in common with the poet though you may not have realised. It is the belief in symbols. You believe that beneath the symbol is a language that can be deciphered and read and that in reading you will discover the truth. Isn't that so? The same is true of the poet, only their canvas is much broader: it encompasses all aspects of life and death.

How do I know, Detective? I know in the same way I know you are a widower. By *seeing*. Don't look so surprised. All black. A ring you never touch or even glance at but insistently wear. The starved appearance. If you're not a widower then I didn't kill those girls in Houston. And you know I did it, don't you Detective Rogers?

Would you like to know how?

Of course not! You already know how. You've read the symbols.

You've dug like a fox through every garbage can, gutter, and shit-heap in Texas to find the pieces to your mental picture. I bet you can see how I did it like you were really there. I bet you even dream you're me sometimes, doing it. Over and over.

No, what you really want to know is *why*. What it all meant.

Well, you're in luck, Detective Rogers. I'm going to tell you. I want everyone to know. My gods have spoken. I am their mouthpiece.

<>RECORD SUSPENDED</>

Day 1

26th December 2067

Prisoner 360 lay in a lightless room and dreamed of a portal shimmering in the deep of space.

The portal was not visible in the way that other things were visible. It contained only two dimensions and yet somehow *inside* the flat circle a kaleidoscope universe stretched and unfurled into an illimitable distance that seemed to encompass time as well as height and width and depth. It was into these realms the prisoner stared.

Within the infinite kaleidoscope he could see seven shapes: shapes that glared with knowing intent out at the starless expanse and were not afraid. Each one was subtly different and yet all of them seemed to be an expression of a greater darkness that he couldn't see, as though they were all the children of one father.

The portal hovered towards him and he could see the shapes more clearly though he could never look at them full on. One looked like a slender lord with a crown. Another was like a pregnant spider. A third had a dark, curved horn protruding from the centre of its head that cut across eternity like a black scar, gargantuan enough to split worlds. The prisoner felt terror as they drew nearer but his terror was overwhelmed by excitement that his purpose might at last be fulfilled. He had waited for this moment for so long and he prayed everything he had done, all the trials that had taken over his life, would finally come to fruition.

He floated in the dark expanse. The portal, though flat, seemed to bend and wrap around him; it began to spin as if caught in his gravitational pull. Each shadow in the flat surface flashed at him, scarring across his retina like sunlight. The reflection of the shaded world made him dizzy, as though his brain was turning over and over inside his skull like a restless sleeper.

'Let me come to you,' he croaked.

In speaking he realised he had no spacesuit, no oxygen. He choked and gripped his throat. Coldness flushed across his skin like a sudden leprosy. Laughter erupted around him and the glimmering portal shattered – made only of brittle glass. The shards pierced him, drove deep, like fingers tipped with nails long as swords. Pain. So much pain. He looked up from his gaping wounds and stared into a face with a crown like a jagged black skyline.

It's almost time.

Craig Smiley opened his eyes.

He breathed into the root of his stomach and listened. The four blank metal walls throbbed with an electrical pulse like blood through the veins of a leviathan. It was not the first time he had dreamed that dream but he hoped it was the last. The gods mocked him. Why couldn't they let him see? He had done everything they asked. Everything they asked and more. Why hadn't it been enough?

He stood and stabbing pain drove through the tops of his feet. The implants had been inserted there seven years ago but some days they hurt just as bad as the first. They were at once tracking devices and magnets that could be activated at any moment in order to pin him where he stood. All the inmates had them, but Smiley guessed his were the only ones that were monitored daily.

The klaxon that began his day sounded a harsh call through the prison. An electronic buzz followed it and the door to his cell slid open. Two guards clad in full body armour appeared at the door. They wore glass-visored helmets with in-built oxygen breathers and carried heavy calibre automatics in their hands. Couldn't have government employees breathing the same shit as the inmates. On Earth the guns would have been too heavy to heft around, they were more suitable for entrenched positions, but on Mars the lower gravity meant they could be carried around and used like a standard machine gun. Smiley estimated they fired roughly 40. to 44. calibre bullets: easily capable of cutting him in half.

'Gym, 360,' one said.

He nodded and stepped out into the corridor and held out his hands in front of him. One clapped handcuffs around his wrists and the other placed a pair around his ankles so he could only shuffle along.

'Move.'

The prison was shaped like a cylinder and had been drilled into the crust of Mars. For the most part it was hollow, without oxygen and subject to the atmosphere of Mars. The cylinder roof was capped with a jaw-like pair of blast doors and at its bottom there was a pair of blast doors which led to a docking bay beneath. The hollow interior allowed freight, supply ships and GCs to dock more easily. The ships would fly into the hollow cylinder and the first set of blast doors would seal, flooding the chamber with oxygen stored in one of the prison's generators. From there the ship could descend to the docks below. Those doors then sealed and the chamber would decompress, the oxygen presumably recycled into the rest of the facility, allowing the outer atmosphere to enter again. It had been one of the greatest innovations of the 2040s, the discovery of how to harvest the particle-sized oxygen contained in Mars's deep mantle.

Smiley looked through the rad-resistant window in time to see a large freight ship descend through the upper blast doors into the cylinder. As he rounded a bend he lost sight of it.

The cells ringed the outer edge of the prison and were linked together by sealed corridors and stairs. The lower gravity of Mars gave rise to issues with elevators and so there were none. Every level could be sealed individually by blast doors to which only the prison wardens held the keys. He passed under three on his way to the morning gym.

The floors were metal. The walls were metal. The stairs were metal. The entire thing had been constructed like a machine built to dehumanise the prisoners into apes and it was a gloriously effective system.

He stepped through a doorway into a long, thin gymnasium lined with weights, treadmills and filled with sour inmates who looked at Smiley as he entered. He felt their eyes judge him, accuse him, perhaps more vehemently than even his captors. He grinned at them. Murderers and rapists and felons meant nothing to him. Only those who did what they believed in meant anything to Craig Smiley.

'Your sixty minutes starts now,' a guard said. He stood by the wall, finger casually on the trigger, eyes never leaving him. 'Don't talk to the others.'

He'd tried that before of course. He knew they were frightened by the power he had over people and they didn't want him breaking the machine they'd so meticulously built. He was not like the other savages in Facility Six: inbred tattoo-toting cock-sucking monkeys banging on the bars of their mental prisons whilst herded about their real one by the zookeepers who called themselves prison wardens, zookeepers who were not very much more intelligent than them. Of course he did what he had to do like the rest. He pretended to be an eggshell with the yoke scooped out of it. But he was not like them.

He sat himself down on a bench and picked up a single-handed weight. On Earth he used 5kgs but on Mars he was lifting 13 kg with ease. He watched the inmates. There was a subtle dance going on in the precious minutes of freedom from their cells. He was sure the guards knew about it but turned a blind eye. He watched one wraith of a man sidle up to the dreadlocked giant Rusty and slip something into his pocket while he lay bench-pressing an obscene weight. They called him Rusty because his skin was reddish brown and because his face looked like it was in a state of decay. Still, he was the best of the many traders in Containment Facility 006. The inmates traded everything, including their bodies. Though every freight ship was checked somehow razors and cigarettes found their way into the hands of the desperate or well connected. The prison wardens didn't stop them smoking. If they wanted to poison their own oxygen supply, so be it. Craig Smiley knew they'd already mixed in a calming agent into the oxygen they pumped in to placate them all. He could taste it with every sickening lungful. Perhaps that partly contributed to how easily their riots were quashed?

The guard called his time. An hour had blinked past. As Smiley turned to go he caught Rusty's eye. The giant glared at him, his grizzled, sunken face giving him the aspect of an old-testament prophet. His huge arms were folded across his chest. He closed his eyes as if he couldn't bear to look at him.

The guards pushed Smiley back inside his cell and it shut with an angry buzz. He sat down cross legged in front of one of his bare, markless walls and began to punch it with everything he had.

It was the only way he knew to combat the numbing effect of the compound in their air supply. He punched until his knuckles bled and recited every deed the prison wardens had done to him over and over again like a fell prayer until he felt so much poisonous anger he thought he'd throw up his guts. Among his murderous recitation were the names Tom Marvin and Caleb Rogers.

After he was finished he sat in the dark and held his shattered hands and stifled a scream. For all his faith sometimes he wondered whether he would ever get out, would ever see sunlight, would ever roam over the crags of a mountain and taste blood in his mouth and feel the power of the living gods. He knew he was being tested but he had no concept of when this test would end.

Another klaxon. Again, two guards appeared. They took him down to the mess hall and sat either side of him while he ate, or rather drank, the vitamin-pumped fuel that constituted his daily bread.

'Mucus in a carton,' he said, with a smile the guards ignored. 'Never gets old.' He raised it as if in toast and gulped it down.

Just as he was about to leave the wraith he'd seen earlier with Rusty drew a shiv from his belt and plunged it into the back of a muscle bound bruiser. Blood spurted out in a single jet. The bruiser stood up and pulled the knife out of his back and the wraith backed away trembling.

'NOW I'M GOING TO CUT YOU YOU FUCKING FAGGOT.'

The guards stood and shouted a halt but the bruiser was so enraged he picked up the wraith by the neck and began ramming the knife again and again into his gut until his intestines were hanging out of the ripped sack that'd once been a stomach. Then he turned the shiv of random inmates around him, blood-drunk.

'So much for your compound,' Smiley said, as the guards began firing warning shots. They rushed into the throng. Five more appeared from the other side of the canteen and piled into the cluster with tasers and batons.

Smiley thought the hubbub would keep them occupied for at least another five minutes. Quiet as a panther he stood and walked over to a table where Rusty was sitting alone.

'I've got nothing for you, Smiley,' he said, before he'd even sat down.

'You haven't heard what I have to offer,' he replied, sitting.

Rusty snorted.

'Yeah I have. The whole damn prison has heard about your religious bullshit. Where've your gods been these last seven years Smiley? Probably tired of talking to a shit-piece like you.' He laughed and took a long puff on a cigarette whose paper was yellow and wrinkled as parchment. 'The only thing you might have been good for is as a bitch to fuck but none of us going to go near you. You wanna know why?' He puffed again, fast and angry, and pointed at Smiley. 'Because you're dead sick and we don't wanna catch it. Sick in the head.' He tapped his temple with his index finger as though trying to drill through to the skull. 'The things you did to them girls: no reason for doing shit like that. No reason at all.' He spat. Smiley felt saliva splatter his chin. He was repulsed by its smell. 'Fuck your religion,' Rusty said.

Slowly, Smiley raised his hand to his chin and wiped the spit from his face.

'It's not about religion. It's about purpose.'

The trader's eyes narrowed.

'Get the fuck away from me man.'

'Why? You worried the sickness will catch even if you don't put it up me?'

'I'll break you!' Rusty growled and stood, cracking the knuckles at the ends of his bear-like arms. The scars on his face made a kind of maze design Smiley found fascinating.

'You can't break me...' He whispered. 'Because I'm not even real. I'm in your head.'

'Get away from him now! Now!'

Craig Smiley stood and raised his cuffed hands. He shuffled around the bench, backing away from Rusty. Rusty sat back down slowly but his eyes were over-bright and shifted left and right. The guards grabbed Smiley's shoulders and thrust the nozzles of their automatics into his kidneys.

'What did you say to him? What the fuck did you say to him?'

He smiled to himself on the inside. As if it mattered what he said really. It was how he said it.

They threw him down and beat him with the butts of their guns until he bled from his nose and mouth on the floor. He felt almost no pain in his body, but in his mind a dull throbbing ache woke as though blood clotted somewhere in his brain. He saw a gut-strewn field, citadels in which only ash rained, and he saw Private Jack Fender guttering on his own blood as the Korean soldiers kicked him again and again and again.

He came to in his cell and was glad of the stark walls and the near-silence and the emptiness. Those days in the war against Korea had eternally been filled with sound and sights that could tear a man's sanity open like a tin can and spill every last filthy madness contained within. He had been a different person then. Conditioned. Lobotomised. Like the rest of them. The mind-breaking military conditioning was not so different from the practices used inside the very prison he was in now to produce empty drones. But the terror of the war had set him free from his training: And when he had been set free, he had become something else. He felt it.

He sat up and began counting.

Only one miserable routine remained in his day. At 15:00 he was allowed a twenty minute walk accompanied by four armed guards and was relocated to his cell at 15:20 without fail. The prison warden Hank Marshall called it 'walkies'. Craig Smiley called the prison warden the stupidest cunt alive. Unlike the guards who worked out 4 hours a day to maintain their strength for if they ever returned to earth, the prisoner's bodies were only exercised enough to keep them from serious illness.

Smiley counted the minutes and the hours until 15:00 running over the facts and dates in his head, keeping himself mentally agile. It was the twenty-sixth of December, the first day of the Nemontemi, and the year was 2067. Seven years since he'd been incarcerated.

It was so easy to lose track of time on Mars. There were no clocks in the cells and the prison wardens never stated the time they ate or got to shit or had to exercise because they wanted the inmates to become disorientated, to lose themselves. Human rights initiatives would call it a form of torture but since the crises of the 2020s all the movements advocating criminal rights had gone out of the window save the abolition of the death sentence. How deeply ironic it was.

The warden Hank Marshall was stupid enough to wear a watch showing earth-time. It'd occurred more than once to Smiley the warden was like an actor who asks for a line prompt: he'd made the single gesture which shattered the whole grand illusion. Every day Smiley reminded himself what day it was by looking at Hank Marshall's watch and counted down one more day towards some indefinite point he knew was coming though he wasn't quite sure when.

The klaxon.

Time for walkies.

The warden and two guards were waiting for him outside the cell. Hank Marshall was a short man with a beer-gut that looked like it was about to detach from his body and form a second globular being. He had a neck so thick a bull would have been proud of it. His appearance combined with the fact he jangled as he walked (he had a master-belt of keys and a hobby in collecting army knives) led to the nickname Santa.

Hank grinned at him.

'Oh these boys busted up that face of yours didn't they? Not that it was pretty before.'

Smiley didn't rise to the bait. He stood between the two guards and allowed them to cuff his wrists. They walked like a funeral procession down the bending corridor. Smiley saw on Hank's watch the time was 15:01. At 15:20 a guard would check his cell to make sure he was back in there. The warden swaggered with his hands in his pocket. Smiley felt revulsion. Ignorance was the sin he tolerated least.

'I've been thinkin' lately,' Hank began. 'Thinking real hard.'

'Don't strain yourself.'

Hank looked at him with a snarl. For all his stupidity and flab there were tendons standing out in his neck that made Smiley think of steel cables. The inmates often talked about what the warden had been before he was the warden. Smiley never participated in these conversations but he listened. Some said once he'd been a marine. Maybe he and Smiley even fought in the same damn war. If they had, Hank had learnt nothing from it at all, unlike Smiley.

'I wouldn't want to see you get beat again now.'

'Whatever you say.'

Smiley met his stare with blank indifference. Hank chewed, sniffed and turned his eyes away from him onto the corridor floor, satisfied.

'So, I've been thinking lately about your place here. I think you've been a good boy recently. So we're going to move you to a nice quiet place all by yourself where you won't have to go to the gym or eat in the canteen or put up with the others inmates. I know that can be rough.'

'Solitary confinement.'

Hank grinned and showed teeth, half of which were slightly undersized which told Smiley they were false.

'No you've got it all wrong. We're helping you out. Doing you a favour.' Hank swivelled on his heel and stopped. The guards halted abruptly. The warden walked up to Smiley until they were nose to nose. 'I know you're a religious man, Smiley. You gotta' pray. So you won't have to do gym time anymore. You won't have to do these walks either. Bet you're glad about that, aren't you? You can pray as much as you like and no one is gonna' bother or hear you.' Hank looked into his eyes as though searching for a crack in a fortress. Smiley offered nothing. Hank bared his teeth. 'You're going to – what do the doctors call it? – *atrophy* until you're nothing more than skin and a sack of bones bleeding shit. And you can beg your gods all you want but they ain't gonna' save you. You know why?' He leant in even closer. Smiley smelt whiskey on his breath. He didn't flinch or turn away. He felt Hank's finger press into his chest. 'Because they ain't real. And if they were, they're punishing you for what you did to them girls.'

Smiley smiled.

'No they're not. *You're* punishing me for what I did to those girls, warden.'

Hank stepped back and snorted. A small smile hitched up the corners of his lips.

'I've got to hand it to you Smiley. You are a genuine psychopath, aren't you? Scared of nuthin.'

If only you knew, Smiley thought.

'I'm scared of lots of things, warden.'

'Yeah? Like what?'

'Spiders.'

Hank laughed, it was a long, loud, ringing laugh that chased itself around the corridors.

'I can't believe this. You pulling my leg?'

Smiley shook his head.

'Do you know why, as a species, we have a fear of spiders?'

Hank swivelled and started walking. The guards each put a hand on his shoulder and pushed him on.

'Didn't they tell you in third grade dipshit? It's evolution. One of our ancestors got bitten and remembered what it did to him and passed it down. Plain as...'

'But it's not the poison we're scared of,' Smiley said. 'We put poison inside ourselves aplenty. In fact, I can smell the poison on you right now, warden. It's the shape of the spider we fear: the way it moves, the blank alien buds of its eyes, the slouching pregnant body it heaves behind it, laden with pale, ghostly young. Phantom children. It is the shape that wakes the Prime Fear in us. This fear is rooted so deep in us we forget it's there until something reminds us of it. It's a fear of the cosmic gods.'

Smiley spoke with rapture in his voice, his eyes widened to look past the metallic walls of the prison and into a dim future only he could guess at. He looked catatonic and yet inside his eyes a life danced more vital than that of anyone that'd ever lived.

Hank narrowed his eyes.

'What the fuck are you talking about?'

'The Eight Legged Queen.'

Hank burst into a rasping laugh.

Hank Marshall started laughing so hard he bent over where he stood and clutching his belly, silent tears rolling down his face. Smiley felt his teeth grind together.

'Hank,' one of the guards said, with warning.

'I know,' Hank spluttered. 'I know we got to be back in time it's just – can you believe this guy? Wooo.' He slapped his cheeks and took a breath, still chortling. 'It's a shame we're going to be putting you away. I won't get to hear anymore of –'

All the lights went out.

They froze in the stunned silence.

Craig Smiley stood in the total darkness and started to tremble. He felt as though he'd been dropped into inky waters. Time slipped away from him, shedding like a skin until there was only the stark blankness of space. He heard seven voices whispering in his ear and felt Mars falter in its rotation as the starscape ground to a halt before turning and spinning in the other direction. Each star blinked as though a glowing eye.

He knew at that moment, in the urgent darkness, the order of the cosmos had changed.

He smiled.

Lurching to the right he seized the guard's trigger hand on the heavy calibre weapon and squeezed the finger whilst swinging his body around. An arc of yellow light like the fizzle of a dimming star cut through the blackness and he heard Hank and the other guard scream as the 44 rounds blew holes in their bodies with a patter-patter sound. He heard them hit the ground just after.

The guard tried to get his hands around Smiley. Smiley thrust his elbow back, snapping it into his throat. The guard spluttered and staggered back, letting go of him. Smiley manoeuvred his feet nimble and light as a dancer so he stood behind him. He threw the chain between his handcuffs around the guard's neck and pulled. The guard roared and threw himself back, slamming Smiley against the wall, but he didn't slacken his grip. The guard flailed, coughed, punched. Smiley held on. He felt the body twitching and jerking against him in the dark like furtive lovemaking. He was aroused. He tightened the grip. He felt the warm liquid run down the inside of his arms. The guard groaned and went limp. Smiley kept squeezing. You had to be sure.

Then the guard fell down with a thumping noise and the lights flared into being as though ignited by the offering. They'd been off no longer than thirty seconds. The other guard lay sprawled in the corridor, the visor exploded inwards, blood and brain spilling from a hole in his face that bored through to the back of his head. Hank Marshall lay gasping on the floor clutching his shoulder. A chunk the size of an apple had been taken clean out of it and there was another wound in his thigh. Blood was everywhere.

'You...You bastard...' he stammered, looking half crazed. It was amazing how quickly things could change, Smiley thought. 'Wait there. Wait there damn you. Guards! Guards!'

Smiley walked over to him, slow as a cat stalking its bleeding quarry. *Yell all you want to, you stinking piece of shit.* He bent down and picked a key off the master-belt and unlocked his cuffs. Then he reached inside Hank's pocket and seized his wallet, a security card and an army knife. He took off Hank's watch and put it on his own wrist. The time was 15:18. He had two minutes.

'You'll never...'

Smiley slapped him, the smallest smile on his face. Hank whimpered. His eyes flitted to the other heavy calibre gun. Smiley picked it up and carried it out of reach, tutting.

Smiley crouched and flicked out the army knife and put it to the top of his feet. For some, this might have been the hard part, but Craig Smiley was afraid of pain no more than he was of solitary confinement. He had seen things in the war against Korea, or rather, been shown things, that could destroy minds.

He stabbed the blade down into the foot and forced it down until it touched metal, grimacing. Then he twisted it, pushed in at an angle, and drove the blade's tip under the magnetic implant. He wrenched up and the metal flew out and pinged across the corridor. He did the same with the other foot. He stood shakily, feet punctured and bleeding like the feet of that false Christian god. Smiley grinned at the irony of it.

The first guard's suit was too shot-up to be of any use, so he went to the guard he'd strangled and quickly stripped him and donned the visored oxygen mask and took up the heavy calibre gun. The taste of clean air almost made him nauseous. He thumbed the release catch of the machine gun and the magazine slid out. He checked it then slapped it back in and slid the bolt so the first bullet notched into place with a smooth click. Twenty years and his muscle memory functioned just as smoothly as the weapon itself.

He took one of the radios off the guard's belt and glanced at the watch. 15:19.

'You'll never escape,' Hank said. 'Never.'

Smiley walked over to him and bent down and pushed his finger into Hank's wounded shoulder. The warden screamed. Smiley withdrew his finger and walked over to one of the windows, Hank groaned as though in the throes of a dark sleep. Smiley began to draw. When he was done painting he stepped back and looked at it. He imagined Caleb Rogers and Tom Marvin being sent after him and finding the symbol drawn onto the wall. He imagined their faces. Their despair. Everything they'd worked on for two years to put him away undone. He knew Caleb would be a broken man. The thought brought another disturbing smile to his face, the smile of an angler fish beneath sickly light.

He looked at Hank Marshall.

'I've already escaped.'

He turned and started running down the corridor, a spirit pursued by the chariots of the death-god Anubis.

Right on cue, sirens blared throughout the facility.

Three guards came running down the corridor.

'Have you seen Smiley?' one shouted to him. Then his eyes went wide.

Smiley swung the automatic to his shoulder and fired three sharp bursts that sent them crumpling to the floor like boneless creatures, a cloud of red settling over them. In his mind he saw them fall to the surface of a wasteland swept by ash and heard artillery fire coming from the hill. He shook himself. He had to focus on the now.

He ran on. His breaths came faster than his feet pounding the floor, faster than the maddening pulse of his heart which felt like the recoil of a machine gun against his chest. A blast door descended in front of him. He slid and rolled, just making it underneath.

There was a zigzag staircase to his right behind a sealed security door. He went over to it and swept Hank's card across it and the door flashed green and opened. He put a foot on the stair. Up or down? Up lead to the surface but even if he did get there his chances were slim. But if he could get to the docking bay below the blast doors there were ships waiting. He paused and brought the radio to his lips and clicked it on.

'This is Hank Marshall,' he impersonated. 'Prisoner 360 is heading up the staircase on level 6. Repeat, prisoner 360 is on the staircase on level 6 heading up to level 7. Over.'

He started to descend.

The radio fizzed.

'Copy that.'

It crackled and another voice, heavy, ragged.

'It's him! It's him god-damn-it. This is Hank Marshall. He's heading down...'

Smiley had to hand it to him, the warden was tough.

He leapt down the stairs and burst through the security door on level 5. At the far end of the corridor to his right he saw five or six guards coming. On his left there were three more.

Caught like a rat in a maze. He looked around. He had only moments before they came and put an end to him. He saw there was a window set into the wall in front of him and behind it a ship lowering into the cylinder. Something clicked, like a door unlocking.

He fired at the window and it shattered. He ran forward. Gunfire spat around him but it was sluggish and wide of the mark. He leapt and crashed through the broken window.

He fell, tumbling. The wide blast doors opened to receive him like an abysmal mouth.

<>ACCESS LOGS</>
  <>MARS CONTAINMENT FACILITY 006</>
  <>RECORD NO. 101008</>
  <>CREATED 14:12:01 27/12/2060 EARTH TIME</>
  <>BEGIN RECORD</>

SCIENTISTS HAVE SAID that there is a black hole located at the centre of our universe. This may or may not be true. But I think it is a metaphor. Scientists never see the metaphors in life or in their work. They are blind to them.

The universe is a person. And the black hole is their hunger. It is the emptiness that drives us. I call this hunger The Mouth and it is one of the oldest of the cosmic gods.

Now before you ask the question, Detective Rogers, I am not speaking in metaphor.

The reason I killed that girl down in Houston the way I did was to make her a fitting offering to The Mouth. She couldn't hope for a greater honour. Not with her future. She was a prostitute. She sold her dignity and her self-respect. But worse than that she turned her back on *being*. She denied that her life had meaning or purpose. So many people do. It's because they are afraid of responsibility.

I gave her purpose back.

<>RECORD SUSPENDED</>

DAY 120

Caleb stepped down from the GC onto the cold metallic floor of the landing dock and breathed the artificial air with distaste. One quick glance told him not much had changed in this hellhole since last he'd been there.

Waiting for him was a troop of guards in stark blue and white body armour carrying SA101 automatics, guns that were used as trench weapons back on earth. A stocky man in a grey shirt and an oxygen breather limped towards him and handed him his own breather which he strapped on.

'The inmates fill the air with all kinds of shit,' the warden said.

'Is some of that shit nicotine?' Caleb said.

The warden nodded.

Caleb took off his breather.

'Then I'll stick like this for now and let you know if I get dizzy.' He grinned and handed the breather to Tom, who was emerging with the two pilots. In the clinical white light of the docking bay Tom looked unhealthy. Bags rimmed his eyes like eclipses and he moved as though stoned or pissed or both. Caleb guessed interplanetary travel wasn't so good for Tom either.

'Hank Marshall,' the warden said, jerking out his hand.

'Detective Caleb Rogers. We've met once before.'

Although back then Hank Marshall had been a very different man. He'd lost a lot of weight. But the main thing was his swagger was gone. It wasn't just because he was limping. Caleb Rogers could spot a change in attitude quicker than someone's own mother. Before, Hank Marshall had maintained the air of someone who thought pain was for other, lesser people. Now his eyes were rheumy and the lids peeled back to show the red beneath; it gave him a look of constant fear. The fat red cheeks which suggested one too many whiskeys sagged so his face looked long and tired.

'Oh yes,' he said. He forced a smile. Tom stood next to Caleb and extended a hand and the warden shook his.

'Detective Tom Marvin.'

'If you'd like to follow me I'll introduce you to the prison Overseer.'

'Much obliged,' Caleb said.

They followed Hank down a series of identical metal corridors separated by security doors which could only be opened by a card. They were accompanied by a retinue of guards. Considering there were no cells on the docking level, Caleb thought their services would be best employed elsewhere. He barely remembered any of the prison, apart from the inside of the interview room and the hours spent trying to get something from Smiley – he hadn't even been sure what it was and he still didn't know but he'd sensed if he pushed him he might yield some reason or idea or words. Maybe he'd been looking to break Smiley, to make him lose faith. But he never got anywhere close to that. He made him mad a couple of times, got under his skin, but he never scathed the fabric of his belief. It was too strong.

At the end of one corridor he saw a wooden door which looked at complete odds with the rest of the facility. Hank went up to it and knocked.

'Come.'

Hank opened the door and held it for the two detectives, who stepped through. The warden closed it softly behind them. Caleb realised the sound of a wooden door closing was oddly reassuring when you'd been on a metal ship for a hundred and twenty days.

The Overseer's room was also unlike anything else in the facility. A view of a glimmering New York city at night shimmered on a gigantic plasma screen which ran like a stripe round two sides of the room, mimicking a window. An oak table and cabinet stood against the other wall of the room. Caleb felt as though they were meeting on the top floor of an office block rather than 12 floors below ground. There was even sound the sound of soft traffic, wind and sirens being played through invisible speakers to cement the effect.

The Overseer could not have been more different from her office. She was a short, well-built woman in a sleeveless grey shirt which showed arms as quietly muscular as a marine's. Her hair was tied back in a ponytail and her face might have been attractive if not for the two purple gouges that ran across her cheeks and mouth. When she stood abruptly on their entering, Caleb could see power in her movements that could only from relentless, painful training.

She put her hands in her pocket and sighed.

'So, you're the twats who drew the short straws? Shipped all the way to Mars away from your wives for the sake of one prisoner.' She grinned. The scar meant one side of her mouth pulled back slightly further than the other, making it a snarl. 'Not only that, you're four months late. I do salute the stupidity of Command.'

Tom raised an imaginary glass. Caleb's lips twitched.

'Do you drink?' she went on. 'I should offer you one. I don't ever touch the stuff myself but my predecessor could have started a liquor store.' She went to one of the drawers in a cabinet. She pulled out two bottles of dark amber liquid. 'Your poison?'

'Whiskey,' Tom croaked. He took a seat on a cushioned chair. Caleb waved his hand.

'Sensible,' she said, nodding at Caleb. She handed Tom a glass of whiskey. He drained it in one neat jerk of the hand and gave her the empty glass. She put it back on the desk and sat back down. 'I'm Carla Bolton. The inmates call me the killer bitch behind my back. Before you bore me to death with questions I want to make one thing perfectly clear: this facility's been searched top to bottom. Every second of footage of every camera has been watched and re-watched. Every flight log of every supply and freight ship in and out of here has been checked and double checked. We've put out APBs to every colony within 100 miles and not one of them has had word of the prisoner. Internal investigators scoured this place the day after he escaped and found nothing. You want to know why? Because he's a fucking skeleton turning into dust on the surface of Mars, that's why.'

'At least you hope so,' Caleb said.

Carla leant back in her chair and snorted.

'Frank Martin was running the place when Smiley was brought in back in 2060.' Tom began, as though he hadn't heard a word spoken. 'He's left now?'

'That's right.' She put her feet on the desk, pointing the studded soles of military-grade boots in their faces.

'And you came in...?'

'Two years ago. This place was going soft under him. No wonder. He was another rich white patriarch part of the system. He'd lived a life of luxury before his appointment. Unfortunately he was so arrogant he thought he could handle Mars. He ended up drunk half the time. He couldn't hack this planet.' She looked around the room as though she could see Mars all around them. She took her feet off the desk and leant forward. 'Mars is a tough mother. It tries to break you, and if you're not careful, or diligent, it will. It broke old Frank alright. He ran back to Earth with his tail between his legs.' She snorted.

Caleb nodded. There was no agriculture on Mars, just endlessly deep mines and prison facilities – between them miles of red desert. He couldn't think of a bleaker world.

'The prisoner we've come to find, Craig Smiley, we caught and arrested him in 2060 after he'd murdered seven women. He is a dangerous man, even by the standards of the inmates in this prison, and as far as I'm concerned, I'd rather know for sure whether he's dead or alive.'

Carla nodded. She picked up a remote control and clicked a button then pointed to the screen which had changed to show red canyons like something out of the Nevada wilderness. The only difference was the sky hung oppressively low and black as though seeking to envelop and crush any life that might walk its surface.

'Out there, detective, there's nothing but airless desert. Even with the oxygen mask, the body armour he's got doesn't shield against the radiation. He'd get sick before he ever got back to earth. The closest colony is The Iron Caves which is sixty miles.' She shook her head. 'Trust the junkers and smugglers to come up with a fancy name rather than giving it a designation.'

'That may be, but with all due respect, you don't know him like we do. This man has ideals. Some might even call it vision. Men like him find ways of surviving.'

Carla sighed, as though bored.

'What do you need?'

'We need to interview the wardens and any guards stationed on level 6 and any that may have been involved in his escape,' Tom said. 'Was he allowed to speak to any of the inmates?'

'Frank let him mingle, but I saw what he was doing to the inmates: planting seeds of his mind-virus religion in their heads. Stirring shit up. I was having none of it.' Carla looked as though she'd smelt something profane. 'Nothing worse than religion for fucking up your head.'

Tom nodded and shot a glance at Caleb. His face was unreadable.

'Thank you very much for your help,' Caleb said. 'We'll report back to you once we've spoken with everyone.'

She nodded.

'I appreciate you keeping this brief, detectives. I've got five hundred other prisoners that require my attention.'

Tom stood and nodded. He moved to the door and left the office without so much as a thank you. Caleb went to the door after him, but before he followed Tom he turned back to her.

'If he is alive, you're going to have that on your head for the rest of your life.'

She met his gaze with cool ferocity. Her eyes glittered, reminding him of a panther watching with silent but terrible hunger some oblivious prey scamper across its path.

'No I won't,' she said. 'We all make mistakes, detective. I'm sure you've made plenty. I wasn't there the day he escaped.'

Caleb nodded.

'That was your mistake.'

He shut the door quietly.

The first person they interviewed was Hank Marshall, and the interview took place in the same room where Caleb Rogers had questioned Smiley seven years before. Hank seemed to be aware of that fact or else just jittery because he shifted in his chair as though itching a sore and his eyes kept dancing to the camera hovering in the corner of the room.

Tom Marvin leant on the wall, his usual nonchalant pose for such affairs, and Caleb sat directly opposite Hank. Intense. Searching. Caleb was the kind of man who could smell guilt. Hank reeked of it, head to toe. But was it any wonder? He'd let potentially the most dangerous person alive escape from him – and he'd been *there* when it happened. He knew he'd never forgive himself in Hank's shoes.

'I'd tell you to relax,' Caleb said, 'but we both know that's pointless, don't we?'

Hank laughed nervously.

'You bet.'

Caleb sighed. He took out his packet of nicotine gum, popped one in his mouth and chewed.

'The only person we're looking to nail is Smiley.' It was a half truth. As angry as he was he didn't want to let anything distract him from Smiley, but then again, if Hank talked himself into a negligence sentence he wasn't about to leap to his defence. He bored into Hank's mouse-like eyes and thought he could see the writhing soul beneath. Interview was all about how you said it not what you said. 'Take your time. We understand it's been nearly four months since it happened so memory's bound to be a bit hazy. Let's start with the basics.'

'OK.'

'Talk me through Smiley's routine.'

Caleb almost felt sorry for him at first. Hank stuttered through a whole bunch of procedural jargon he didn't give a damn about and used the word 'secure' more times than he could count; but after a while Hank picked up his old way of talking and Caleb remembered why he'd disliked him so much. He talked about the inmates as though they were cattle and Caleb couldn't help but think if he was one of them he'd shank the warden without a moment's hesitation. The inmates were "inbreeds", "ingrates", "scum" and Hank was from a respectable family without a single divorce in four generations; they were "stupid" and Hank was a smart, smart man who'd thought of the idea of equipping the guards with the SA101s which they couldn't utilise on Earth due to their weight. As far as Hank was concerned the inmates wouldn't even dream of escaping because they were afraid he'd follow them across the solar system and beat them shitless. Caleb couldn't believe he'd talk like this even four months on.

'Moving on to the escape – your statement said there was a temporary power outage?'

Hank bit his lip and nodded. He was starting to look nervous again.

'Yeah, some kind of "storm" the technicians said. Shorted out all the lights. Couldn't see a damn thing. Next thing I knew there was gunfire. I went down. He hit me in the shoulder and leg. Bastard's given me a limp that ain't never gonna go away.' He swallowed. Caleb realised the warden was no longer looking at him or the camera but at an empty space in the room, an empty space that was not an empty space but populated by his thoughts. 'He was talking right before it happened. Like...' He looked at Caleb. 'You know what I mean. Talking about his damn gods. He said a name of one of them. A queen or something. And right then – bam – the lights went out. It was like...' He swallowed again as though trying to take a jagged pill. All of a sudden he closed his eyes and slumped back in his chair as though sucked from the world he'd momentarily re-inhabited. 'That's why we kept him apart from the others,' he said. 'Couldn't have him messing with their heads like that.'

'So he was observed all day and every day?' Tom asked.

Hank nodded.

'That's right. We were gunna move him to a new block and solitary confinement, but he got out before then.'

Caleb nodded.

'So he was never allowed to speak to anyone?' Tom pressed again.

Hank shook his head. Tom shot Caleb a glance and the two detectives shared an understanding. Caleb wondered sometimes whether there was something to the claim that people were psychic when he had those moments with Tom, but then again, they'd worked together a long time, of course they could read each other.

'You sure?' Tom said.

'Absolutely.'

Caleb sighed. He stood up and walked until he was standing behind Hank and looked up to the ceiling.

'You're wrong, warden,' he said. 'And you don't even know it.'

Hank swivelled and glared at him. His fist clenched and unclenched on the table like the fronds of a carnivorous plant. So you're not completely beat, Caleb thought, looking at the tendons standing out in his neck.

'With all due respect, detective, you weren't here.'

'You said he was never allowed to speak to anyone.'

'I did and I stand by that statement.' Caleb could hear the breaths hissing from the warden's nostrils like steam.

'Well then, why did you tell us he was speaking *to you*?'

Hank choked on the beginning of a sentence and then fell quiet. Colour drained and he looked like the victim of a vampire's kiss.

'But I...I...'

'You're the warden?' Caleb leaned in until he was nose to nose with Hank. 'You fat arrogant bastard. You thought you could handle him, didn't you? You thought he was just some other dirtbag in the great big kingdom which you've made yourself the king of. Fuck me. How often did you speak with him?'

Hank blinked.

'Every day.'

'Jesus Christ,' Tom said, pushing himself off the wall. He positioned himself on the other side of Hank and put both hands on the table. 'What the hell were you doing?'

'It was his daily walk. I was supervising it...All the prisoners have them!' Hank's voice had raised an octave and he pulled at the collar of his shirt. Caleb could smell his sweat as well as his guilt now and it was worse than the oxygen.

'You know what it looks like, don't you?' Caleb said. He glanced at Tom. 'You thinking what I'm thinking?'

'Sure am,' Tom said, face turning grim. 'Collusion.

Hank looked like he'd been slapped.

'I...'

'Said it yourself,' Caleb snarled. 'You requested the guards have heavy calibre weaponry which the prisoner then used to escape.'

Tom nodded. Hank was looking between the two of them as though waiting for one of them to turn and come to his defence.

'It was so we could keep those bastards down, damn it. You don't know what it's like out here! You don't know -'

'What don't I know? What don't I know, Hank?'

'You ain't been out here long enough to judge me.' The warden's bellow tore from him sudden as a changing wind. He looked on the verge of either a heart attack or a psychotic event.

'And you've been out here too long,' Caleb replied coolly. 'So long you've forgotten what happened on earth. You forgot what Smiley did.'

'I ain't forgotten anything. I know what he did to those poor women. Everyone does.'

'Really?' Caleb said. He circled the warden so he stood next to Tom, who stood with arms crossed. Tom's expression was one of utter disregard, a look that could wither even the most arrogant soul and make it question itself.

'Then tell me what he did to Louise Hurt.'

'She was the prostitute.' He said the word the same way he said the word 'inmate', the same way he'd said Smiley's name. Dismissal, arrogance, negligence. No wonder Smiley had gotten out so easily, Caleb thought, the work had been done for him.

'He remembers that part,' Tom snorted.

'You the champion of hookers now?' Hank growled. 'Thought you were supposed to be cops!'

'And I thought you were supposed to be a prison warden?' Tom shot. Hank went blood red and stood.

'I'm gunna –'

'He pulled out her guts through her mouth.'

Hank froze as though Caleb had pulled off a mask and revealed a Gorgon's face. He swayed stupidly on his gammy leg and his mouth twitched.

Caleb went on.

'He forced a towel down her throat so far her stomach started to digest it and then he pulled. She chewed her own damn organs. And now he's free. 'Cos of you.'

The warden opened and closed his mouth without sound. Slowly, he sat.

'I think you didn't know who the fuck you were dealing with.'

The intimidation had been an act but Caleb found himself too sick and angry to go on with it. For two years he'd stomached darkness no other cop in Texas had ever had to save Tom Marvin and even he didn't swallow the full draught of it. He'd been protected by his atheism in a way. Caleb had been fully open to the meaning and the symbols – just like Smiley had said to him in this very room.

No wonder Martha had talked about divorce so often. How could someone function when they dreamed of dead girls and watched their wife eat every meal as though expecting it to be their last?

After Caleb had caught Smiley everything had been ok for a while, as though a poison had been sucked out of him. He and Martha stayed ok for another two years until the accident.

Thinking about it made him feel faint. He leant against the wall and closed his eyes and breathed the sick air and wished he had that oxygen mask. Tom moved towards Hank and sat on the table edge next to him.

'If you'd bothered to read his files, warden, you'd know Craig Smiley was a soldier before he was serial killer. He fought in Korea in '41 and '42. You remember what happened there, right? You know what that war did to people. Doubt a single man came out of those ash-clouds with a sane thought in his head. But those that did had to be tough. You understand me?' Tom clenched his fist and held it in front of Hank who stared at it as though he'd created fire with his bare hand. 'Harder than fucking *nails*.'

The warden bowed his head. He blinked as though fighting back tears. Caleb opened his eyes and looked at the short fat man in grey and saw someone so worn down by the weight of the past they could hardly stand. He knew that feeling: it was the shadow that stalked him wherever he went and hung over his head every time he woke from sleep and threatened to forbid him to rise. Hank looked like he was about to walk out of that interview room find a washroom stall somewhere and slit his wrists. Enough was enough.

'You didn't know,' he said.

The warden looked up at him. His eyes were hollow.

'You said... you...' The warden rubbed his thigh as though the old wound hurt. He wheezed asthmatically. 'The files...'

'We all miss stuff,' Tom said, getting up from the table.

Hank sniffed and stared.

'So you're not...'

'..going to arrest you? No.' Caleb sighed. 'But you fucked up big time.'

'I know.'

Tom leant in close.

'You can help us make it right.'

The warden nodded fervently.

'Anything.'

Tom looked at Caleb, who was pacing again.

'Full access, Hank. No bullshitting. No bureaucracy. We might need to tear this place apart to find out how he got out.'

Hank cleared his throat and tried to look evenly at Tom.

'You know, he said something just before he ran off. After he shot me. It's been haunting me all this time. He said...he said he'd "already" escaped... what'd he mean?'

'Damned if I know, Hank,' Tom said. 'I'll get you a glass of something.' He moved to the door and slipped out.

Hank looked up to find Caleb staring at him. The detective was silent a long time.

'He meant his mind,' he said, after a while.

Hank looked like he still didn't understand.

Caleb took another gum from the inside pocket of his jacket and put it in his mouth. The gum never quite killed the urge like a real smoke did. He knew it was more than just the drug but the whole ritual of it he needed and the gum took that away. He wondered whether the same addiction lay behind the Smiley's desire to kill only magnified, distorted. How could he ever know?

'We'll need to see his cell and the surrounding level.'

'Of course,' Hank said.

Tom reappeared with a glass of whiskey and one of water. He handed Hank the whiskey and set the water down on the table. Hank took a swig of the whiskey and shook himself like a wet dog. He looked slightly better. He finished the whiskey.

'I'll show you.'

<>ACCESS LOGS</>
    <>PSYCHOLOGICAL CLINIC AUSTIN POLICE DEP. TEXAS EARTH</>
    <>RECORD NO. 652</>
    <>CREATED 18:09:33 12/10/2058 EARTH TIME</>
    <>BEGIN RECORD</>

DETECTIVE CALEB ROGERS. Born August 1st 2015. Served the force seventeen years. Got no fucking idea why I'm here. Well, other than Justin saying counselling's compulsory for someone working a case like this. I say there's nothing you can tell me I haven't already heard from my wife.

Don't mind if I smoke, do you?

Fine.

So what do you want me to say? How depressed I am? How angry this job makes me? Or are you looking for my conspiracy theories and my mad ramblings? Well you'll be pleased to know you can discount the conspiracies at least. It's one man I'm after.

As for the ramblings, I've got plenty of that you could look at.

<>RECORD SUSPENDED</>

Day 40

E leanor Cole sat on top of a pile of empty cargo boxes cleaning the hull of her ship for what must have been the hundredth time and sighed. She'd been a junker pilot for 4 years and business had never been this bad. In fact, bad did not even cover it. Business had virtually stopped altogether. Every off-planet flight had been grounded for over a month and much as Eleanor loved The Iron Caves she was getting sick of living on a red dustball.

There was no true sunrise or sunset on Mars. This threw the colonies into a permanent night life that had no respite. On Earth there always came a point where everyone finally staggered home to bed and the city slept. Not so here. She knew the prison facilities had set their clocks to Earth time and some even adjusted their lights to imitate day and night. There were only 39 extra minutes in the length of a day on Mars compared to Earth but Command had thought that was enough for everyone to start falling out of sync.

The colonies, however, had treated those 39 minutes like a new religion. They had embraced the darkness of space like a long lost mother and hurtled willy-nilly into its chaos. Most people were drunk all the time and there were no set working hours. If you wanted a meeting, you arranged for it to start during any of Mars's 24 and two-third hours and prayed the person you were meeting hadn't been drinking. Then after the meeting you went down to the Rock Biter or the Red Devil and made up for lost hours with whatever substance was available.

'How long do you think before they apprehend this man?'

Jim McLeod reposed next to her dressed in a white and orange chequered shirt, a patterned fedora hat, and boasting sandy facial hair that might have suited a French aristocrat of the 18th century. He leant at a jaunty angle on a red-oak cane topped with a silver design of a wolf's head like some billionaire playboy. He was altogether one of the oddest people Eleanor had ever met. He stood out even amongst the inhabitants of places like the Rock Biter and not just because he was a Brit amongst a colony full of Americans. There was something old-school about Jim. He was like a classic model of car they didn't make anymore.

And that was precisely why she liked him.

He was also surprisingly useful. There were things in Jim's head no search engine or computer could supply.

'Don't know. Must be a real badman to shut everything down like this. I heard the lockdown is planet-wide. That's fucking crazy ain't it?'

'It has the hallmarks of insanity, yes.' Jim pursed his lips. Every day the great docking screen that normally showed departure times flashed up with a pixelated image of a bald and clean-shaven convict. Eleanor thought if she ever saw someone that looked like him she'd shoot first before reporting to the authorities. 'Look on the bright side though,' Jim went on, mildly. 'Business might be bad now, but when the lockdown's lifted you're going to have more cargo than your ship can carry.'

Eleanor laughed.

'True. That's if I have enough credits to last us that long.'

'I guess you don't fancy a drink then?'

'You kiddin'?'

Jim offered an arm as though to a lady in waiting. Eleanor leapt down from the pile of boxes, wiped her dirty hands on her slacks, and looped her arm through his.

The Iron Caves looked like a great festering sinkhole capped by a pair of hellish, dust-caked blast doors. When you stared up from the docks situated at the bottom level, you got the impression of being in the blackened spinal column of a gigantic creature in which parasites had set up home. The actual tunnels which were harvested for their valuable minerals, oxygen and water stretched horizontally out from the spine like a great nervous system. There was something eerily beautiful about the caves. Mars was not barren as they'd thought forty years ago. It was just the fruit it yielded had other properties than satisfying hunger.

When they walked up the spiralling slope to the Rock Biter, Jim often remarked it was almost as though the blast doors were keeping something in, rather than the cosmic radiation out, but then he was a man with poetic inclinations.

'It's like we're all part of one great living organism,' he said, watching the machines probe and chime against an as yet untried slope of black crust whilst the miners shouted and climbed and dug.

'Yeah. One that fucking stinks.'

Eleanor Cole didn't have time for poetic thoughts. She was too busy thinking about how she only had 500 credits left in her account and how she'd missed half a dozen meals in the last few weeks. Command had promised a subsidy for those affected by the lockdown but so far there was nothing showing. The only times the blast doors had opened in 40 days was to admit Mars-internal freight ships to dock. For a few moments starlight beamed down in to their subterranean world and a ship hummed into being, hovering over them like a great, furious hornet. Then the light shut off and once more the acrid white glare held sway. The sight of those stars, momentarily glimpsed, called Eleanor. She'd long ago realised her true home was neither on Earth or Mars, but in the pilot seat of *Penelope*, her junker. Her baby.

Its official designation was Junker-0329 but no junker pilot worth their pay didn't give their ship a name. You ate, pissed, slept, shit, drank and just about everything else on your junker. You relied on it more than on any friend, even one like Jim. If you didn't service your junker and she came apart midway through an interplanetary run you died - head popped open by the vacuum like an overripe fruit.

'We're here, Eleanor,' Jim said, gently.

She blinked. She'd been staring down at the docks sprawled below

them, looking at *Penelope* glistening next to the other ships. She didn't
know how long.

'Sorry.'

'It's ok,' he said. 'She'll be in the air soon enough.'

'Yeah. Come on.'

They walked under a garish neon sign into the Rock Biter.

Inside the bar everything was in tumult. A bartender, a burly man in
a white vest and a black moustache that hung like a horse-shoe over his
upper lip, was lifting a slumped woman from the bar and carrying her to
a seat. A group of surly miners played cards in the corner. Touchscreen
monitors set into the tables showed their credit balance. Eleanor could
tell one of them was about to get cleared out by the other two.

The evening progressed much as expected. Eleanor considered
herself tough to beat in a drinking competition and all the more
dangerous to male competitors because of her size and gender, but Jim
McLeod could also hold his drink. The only evidence the alcohol was
having any effect on him at all was the rosy glow in his cheeks. Jim's
natural preference was for ales and meads – drinks most people considered redundant as they were ancient. Out in the colonies the craze was
for rum and highly processed bottled beer. Jim said the rum harked back
to an older tradition of piracy, but Eleanor thought it was because rum
was cheap and strong and didn't spoil – she also thought its colour and
flavour suited Mars all too well.

They played half a dozen games of cards, though never for credit.
As the hours rolled on, patrons came and went. At one point the bar
was so crammed the bartender was yelling for people to step back from
the bar because someone was getting crushed against it. The room
stank of the bitterness of rum mixed with the narcotic smell of male
sweat. The latter was a smell Eleanor had had to grow accustomed to
in her career as a junker. The room was smoky with greenish exhala-
tion issuing like a dragon's breath from a quartet sitting in the corner,
puffing on flavoured vapour pipes. The synthetic aroma of exotic
fruits mingled with the sharper smells in the atmosphere, making it
sickly.

'Never understood the point of vaping,' she said, swigging a cocktail
that was probably nine parts rum.

'It's about sensation,' Jim replied, with only the trace of a slur. 'Everything nowadays is.'

'It's just a taste.'

'Ritual then!' Jim said, raising his finger as though holding up a divine light. 'People need ritual. It's the cornerstone of addiction and we're all addicted to something.'

'What are you addicted to then?'

Jim twirled his moustache.

'Poetry, of course.' He drank. 'And pretty specimens.'

'You're drunk,' Eleanor said, grinning.

'That, my lady, I am.'

After a few hours, Eleanor and Jim were about to stagger back to *Penelope* when a man in full combat armour entered the Rock Biter. Eleanor saw several hands dart to holsters. Guns were technically banned from the colonies but it was so rare anyone from Command audited them this rule had been ignored. The officials who did visit turned a blind eye and found far more interesting things to look at in the more illicit clubs hidden away in the tunnels themselves.

As the stranger had walked in, there had been a sensation as though sound and time had been sucked out of the atmosphere. Everything stilled. Even the barman stopped wiping a spillage and put a warning hand beneath the bar.

The face of the new intruder was not visible because he wore an old 2K30 helmet with a blacked out visor. The 2K30 was one of the original helmet designs worn by the first astronauts to venture to Mars thirty seven years ago. Why he wore it now was an anathema. His combat armour, by contrast, was a gleaming white and azure modern design.

Perhaps more than anything else, however, there was an aura that entered the room with him. It surrounded his figure like the cloud of an electrical storm. Eleanor was not superstitious but she almost thought she could *see* its tendrils reaching out to touch everyone in the room.

The armoured stranger raised a hand.

'I'm here for one thing...' he said.

The tension reached teetering point.

'BOOZE!' He bellowed.

The room laughed. Attention slid from him like a cloak falling off.

The smokers returned to puffing on their vapours, this time emitting the scent of cinnamon. The gamblers dealt another hand. The barman went on wiping down the bar.

To Eleanor's surprise the man came and sat down between herself and Jim as though an old friend. She shifted uncomfortably and wished she had her own pistol on her. She'd left it on *Penelope*.

'Evening,' he said. He had the kind of voice that demanded attention, like the deep bass notes of music. But the fact the music emitted from a blank, featureless visor that made it ominous.

Jim leant forward and extended a hand.

'I don't believe we've had the pleasure?' he said. His voice was light and civil, but Jim's eyes had the intensity of suspicion. His hand was tight on the wolf's head of his cane. 'Jim McLeod. At your service. And you are...?'

'Hank,' the man in the visor said. 'Hank Marshall.'

He extended his hand and shook Jim's.

'The prison warden?' From the stories Eleanor had heard from the freight pilots about the warden she'd expected someone far less imposing – short, fat, and certainly not gifted with a mellifluous voice. 'What're you doing here?'

'You must be Eleanor Cole and Jim McLeod,' he said, as though he hadn't heard the question. 'I hear you are amongst the best at what you do. I have a proposition for you.'

'What kind of proposition?'

'The kind that makes you rich.'

He took out a credit card and placed it against the touchscreen. A glowing blue display appeared showing a balance of 200,056 credits. Jim spat out his drink. The visored man took away the card.

'I offer you 20,000 now and 20,000 when we arrive. That's 40,000 between you.'

'Arrive?' Eleanor said, weakly.

'On Earth.'

'There's a lockdown on, in case you haven't noticed.'

Hank turned his head and looked around the bar as though becoming aware of it for the first time.

'That's why I came to you: you've not been unwilling to break the rules in the past.'

Eleanor growled and was about to tell him to get lost when Jim cut in.

'Why don't you take off your helmet? I'm sure I recognise your voice. Maybe I'll know the face too.'

A slight pause. Then he reached up and took off his helmet. Eleanor half expected it to look identical to the grainy image on the docking screens but it was nothing alike except maybe in shape. Eleanor had seen a fair few haunting faces in her time but nothing compared to what was in front of her: it was a half-crushed mess of purple scars like venomous lightning. A hermit's tangled beard covered the lower half. His hair was a lank, unwashed mess. He looked like her imagining of Odysseus disguised as a beggar in his own home; *The Odyssey* had been Eleanor's favourite story as a child.

But the eyes were hungry; she had the sensation of meeting the gaze of a cobra hypnotising its prey and thought if she looked too long she would be sucked through them as through a portal into an unknowable world.

'A dangerous prisoner escaped facility 006.' Hank said. 'That's why this lockdown is in place. What you don't know...' He lowered his voice. '...is that they'd already gotten off this rock before the lockdown was put in place. He's headed for Earth right now. If Command had any sense they'd send half a dozen GCs after him but they refuse to acknowledge he's escaped. This is where you come in. I need you to help me get to Earth.'

Quiet fell between them and they listened to the raucous yet muted sounds of the Rock Biter around them. Jim and Eleanor shared a glance. She could tell by his face he didn't trust him, but Jim didn't trust anyone. The one time Jim had had a long term partner he'd been jealous to the point of illness. 40,000 credits was an obscene sum, a sum that filled her mouth with saliva, but also one that raised plenty of questions. She tried to think of one of the stories a freight captain had told her about the warden.

'Hank Marshall, right?' she said.

He nodded.

'One of the freight loaders told me a story about you once. Said you had a thing for the overseer of o-six and got drunk one time and tried it on. That true?' She forced herself to watch his eyes, however uncomfortable it made her.

Hank grinned.

'The Killer Bitch? Carla Bolton?' He laughed. 'I might have tried it on once. How'd you think I got these scars?' He pointed to the ugly mess. 'By the way, my mother's maiden name is Joanna and my date of birth is the twenty fifth of September 2012, in case you wanted to run those answers through a database later on.'

He held her gaze levelly until Eleanor was forced to look away. Her gut squirmed but she forced herself to think of 40,000 credits landing in her account, enough money to fix her financial problems for ten years and revamp *Penelope* while she was at it. From what she knew of the warden he checked out. Sure, there were still a lot of gaps they needed filling in before they took him anywhere but it seemed a real deal. She nodded and looked at Jim. He was leaning forward in his chair with his hands resting on his cane and his chin resting on his hands, a shadow had fallen across his face even under the static white lights making him look ghostly.

'Who's the prisoner,' Jim said.

Hank Marshall smiled.

'Well, if we're going to talk about *him*, I'm going to need a stiff drink.' He stood. 'Can I get you anything? Rum? Whiskey?'

'No thanks,' Jim said.

'Rum and coke,' Eleanor said. Hank nodded and moved off towards the bar cutting a path through the crowds who eyed his armour as though it was barbed.

'He's drawing attention to himself and yet he wants to slip under the radar,' Jim said. 'Surely if he was tracking a criminal undercover he'd go in common clothes?'

'But would we have believed him?' Eleanor said.

Jim sighed.

'I suppose not.' He drained the last of his spirit and smacked his lips. He slammed the glass down hard on the table and wiped the back of his mouth with his sleeve. Eleanor thought that was one of the most aggressive displays she'd ever seen in Jim. She put a hand on his arm.

'What's wrong?'

He struggled with word for a moment; his eyes moved as though searching for a handhold in a sheer face of rock. Then he blurted out his answer, like spitting out poison.

'I can't stop this feeling...' He touched his chest. 'It's like... my entire being is in tumult. It's hatred.' He looked at Eleanor. 'I hate him and I don't know why and I feel awful. But I can't stop. I'm just, repulsed.'

Before Eleanor could say anything Hank reappeared with a glass of rum and coke and a bottled beer.

'You know,' Eleanor said. 'The freight captain said you were a whiskey man.'

Hank's smile only widened.

'You know what I've learnt, Captain Cole? Never try to guess what somebody's going to do. People always surprise you.'

<>ACCESS LOGS</>
  <>PSYCHOLOGICAL   CLINIC   AUSTIN   POLICE   DEP.
TEXAS EARTH</>
  <>RECORD NO. 654</>
  <>CREATED 07:30:11 13/10/2058 EARTH TIME</>
  <>BEGIN RECORD</>

WE FOUND ANOTHER VICTIM. He burned her alive the night before
last. He did it not five miles from Nails Creek State Park. A *public* park,
Doc. She hadn't been gagged. That area's all water and flatlands. They
must've heard her screaming for miles and no one went to help. No one
answered her prayers. Makes me wonder if anyone's ever going to come
and answer my prayers when I'm screaming in agony.

Anyway, Tom thinks he's making statements now, playing games,
trying to show us he can do anything anywhere. I disagree. I think it's
more than that. You know underneath we found this little placard. He'd
painted words on it.

'Look at the Radiant God and you shall burn'.

Religion. That's what this is. Or art. There's a deeper spiritual
meaning to his work -

No, Detective Marvin is not religious.

Yes, I do consider it a mark against him.

<>RECORD SUSPENDED</>

DAY 120

'So then he ran down here, used my security card to get through the door.' Hank coughed. He was red faced behind his oxygen mask and under Caleb's stare.

'Continue.'

'Tried to throw us off the scent by radioing in and giving some misdirection but luckily I was able to crawl to the radio hanging on Farley's belt. Then he came out here...' Hank Marshall stopped and pointed both hands parallel towards a window pane as though drawing an imaginary railway track. '...shot through the window and jumped.'

'Jesus.' Tom walked up to the shining new glass pane and peered down the cylindrical space to the jaw-like blast doors below. 'Quite a fall.'

'Lower gravity,' Caleb said.

'Don't surprise me he jumped. My boys were firing at him and would have had him cornered in another few seconds if he hadn't gone through.' Hank scratched his head. 'I don't think I'll ever understand how he moved so quick though.'

'He was a soldier,' Tom said, still peering down. 'He was trained to make decisions in split seconds and then live with them.'

Caleb paced the corridor looking at the walls as though expecting to find a fresh bloodstain. If he closed his eyes he almost thought he could see it: the dream-haunting face of his worst enemy.

'I think we need to up the dose of sedative in this air supply,' Hank muttered.

'It probably wouldn't have made a difference. I don't think it's possible to sedate someone like Smiley.'

Hank licked his lips and frowned.

'You almost sound like you admire him.'

Caleb looked at him. Hank wasn't the first person to say that and it unsettled him every time someone did. Was there a part of him that found such resourcefulness compelling? He pushed it aside. Two years of work to put him away and a stupid fat prison warden had undone it all. He breathed into his solar plexus.

'I think we need to see his cell.'

Cell 360 looked like any of the others.

'I half expected demonic runes,' Tom said. Even Caleb snorted with laughter.

'That reminds me,' Hank mumbled, bring out a handheld touch-screen device. 'I have something to show you. Don't think this was put in the original report we filed. He drew this...with...in blood.'

He held up the screen which showed a picture of the one of the windows on an upper level. It was daubed with an ugly, sprawling symbol drawn in red. Caleb trembled as he reached out and took the handheld from Hank. He examined the picture as though studying it for evidence of forgery. Tom looked over his shoulder.

'Any ideas?'

'Many,' he said.

At one angle it was a dark wheel, like a grinding millwheel or the cog of a grim, ancient engine. The spokes stretched out past the wheel's rim to form spikes that looked like the scythed horns of a rhino attached to a disc. If he looked at it from another direction it also seemed to resemble a bloody spider's web. It could have been a thorny crown in one light but there was also the shape of a portal. At the centre of the portal shone a bloody spot that could have been an eye or could have been a mouth. The portal was different to the other shapes in that it seemed to lie *behind* them and draw them into itself; at once annihilating and unifying; eliminating the shadowy possibilities of what the symbol could or should be and at the same time completing it, like the last piece of a jigsaw. He counted the spokes.

'It's a seven pointed star,' he said.

'Seven murders. Seven years. Seven whackjob gods if I remember rightly.' Tom ran his hand through his hair. Caleb knew it was his nervous tick. He handed back the screen.

'Have that sent to my computer.'

Hank nodded and pocketed the handheld. Caleb took a last look around the cell but found nothing except the odd scratch marks. He, like Tom, had expected writing or art or symbols of some sort and was more disconcerted by their absence.

Hank locked the cell behind them and he stood in the corridor in silence breathing the foul air. He imagined what it would have been like for someone like Smiley, someone full of ideas, albeit, sick and misguided ones. Day in day out for seven years. Caleb could barely stand the place already.

When Caleb came out of his reverie Tom was talking to the warden.

'I'll need access to the CCTV footage all around the facility and logs for all freight ships.'

'Of course,' Hank blustered. 'Of course.'

'And I'll need to interview any inmates that may have had contact with Smiley.' Hank opened his mouth as though about to protest. Caleb cut in. 'I'm not saying you let him off the leash but if one of them overheard him planning something we need to hear it.'

Hank nodded.

'I'll get you an interview with Rusty. They shared gym time and a couple of my boys pulled the two apart at mealtime once.'

Caleb nodded. Tom gave him a look which Caleb had no trouble reading: Hank's working awful hard to get back in our good books. Caleb returned one with a shrug: Of course he is, he's guilty.

'I'll have one of the guards escort Tom to Records and Surveillance,' Hank rambled. 'Regulations and all that. Can't have non-facility personnel go anywhere unaccompanied.' Hank radioed in for the guard. A few minutes later a bulky looking man in combat armour appeared carrying an SA101.

'Right this way,' he said to Tom and proceeded to march down the corridor. Tom shot Caleb a grin over his shoulder which told him he found the whole thing ridiculous. And it was. Hank and his men watched two detectives like hawks and yet they couldn't find one of their own inmates.

Hank took Caleb down the 5 levels of staircase back to the interview room and told him to make himself comfortable. Thirty minutes later they brought in a gigantic dreadlocked inmate. He immediately saw why they called him Rusty. His skin was the colour of the surface of Mars. Unlike most inmates he eyed Caleb with the kind of calm that might be expected from a wildcat just before they pounce. Two guards sat him down in a chair opposite Caleb. Against Rusty, Caleb looked dwarfish, a David contending with Goliath, but the detective's own even stare did not falter under the glowering inmate.

He got out his tablet, keyed in his security code, and then brought up the file on Rusty. His real name was Ben Marlowe. He'd been a junker before he got locked up but was put inside for murdering his boss. Caleb could relate to that. There were days when Justin Walker seemed to exist for the sole purpose of ruining people's lives. Sometimes Caleb wondered whether he related a little too much to the criminals he was supposed to be against but other times he thought that was his greatest strength. He thought like one.

'You smoke?' Caleb said.

Rusty stared at him.

'I said: do you smoke?'

'Yeah,' Rusty said, as though waiting for a bear-trap to close on him.

Caleb pulled out a pack of cigarettes and a lighter.

'One-hundred and fifteen days on the GC and couldn't smoke. Torture man.' He lit it and puffed. Then he tossed Rusty the packet and the lighter.

Rusty looked at him without picking them up.

'So when's the bad cop coming in?'

Caleb burst out laughing.

'The bad cop is in surveillance looking through CCTV. We ain't interested in cracking you Rusty. In a way, we ain't interested in you at all.'

'Why am I here then?'

Caleb drew a long deep breath of smoke. He felt its acid in his lungs, felt the burning at the top of his mouth like a dry kiss, then let it out in one steady stream of smog. They'd tried so hard to find alternatives to cigarettes. E-lights. Vaping. None of it compared to the real thing.

'Smiley,' he said. 'Smiley.'

Rusty snorted.

'I ain't got time for him.'

'You didn't get on?'

Rusty gave him a look as though he'd just dropped his pants and started twirling his cock around in the interview room.

'Could anyone *get on* with him? You retarded?'

'I take it not then.'

Rusty leant across the table.

'You don't know what the fuck you're talking about, do you? If you'd ever met this guy –'

'I have,' Caleb said, with quiet force. 'Actually I'm the one who put him away. And I'm going to put him away again.'

He puffed again and closed his eyes.

'I'll never forget the day. It was mostly a day of waiting. Patience and brooding hand in hand. Something felt different like the air had changed taste. I was waiting for this lens to drop over my eyes and give everything new colour, new perspective. I was looking at the minutiae all the time. The words he painted on those boards underneath his "offerings", the wheres and the whens and the hows, trying to predict what the next one would be or find some spot that formed his base of operations. We must have broken into half a dozen homes in just a few months. We had helicopters flying over for heaven's sake. And then it came to me.' Caleb drew a long invisible line with his finger on the table. Rusty watched, mesmerised. 'He wasn't living anywhere. He didn't have any possessions. All his killing was done with tools and materials on site and that's why some of them were so damn slapdash. This was not a professional man, it was a resourceful one. A shadow on the roadside.

'So that's where we went. We put out patrol cards on every road from Austin to Houston. We caught him at a damn gas station of all places. Had the body of the seventh girl in the car. She wasn't dead when we found her.' Caleb swallowed and took another puff. 'Had a crown of barbed wire pushed into her scalp so deep she was delirious, brain damaged. She died in hospital.'

'For real?' Rusty said.

'For real.'

Caleb gathered himself.

'So, you're going to tell me what you know about Smiley. If you do, you can keep the damn cigarettes.' A thought occurred to him. 'Or sell them on. I'm guessing you trade?'

'Smiley draw on you when you took him?'

'You mean did he resist arrest?'

'Yeah.'

'No. He just said: It's finished.' Caleb gritted his teeth. He remembered the terrible grin on Smiley's face and the glint in his eye as he held up his hands. For a moment Caleb had wanted to pull the trigger anyway. Fuck protocol. But then he'd found himself twisting Smiley's hands behind his back and cuffing him, the red and blue lights of the squad car like some throbbing aurora around them. He shook himself. Rusty was watching him.

'You trade?'

'Everyone trades in o-six,' Rusty said. 'Except Smiley. No one would deal to him. At first he got to working on people and they believed the shit that came out of his mouth. After a while people got wise to it though. His religion and shit. Ain't no place for that here. I killed my boss because he was a prick. I'd never do no harm to girls like that. That's messed up.'

Rusty picked up a cigarette and lit up.

The rest of the interview ran smooth as a river. Rusty told Caleb pretty much everything he could though large parts of it he knew already. He inquired in details about the altercation at the canteen and what was said. Rusty admitted it was four months ago and some of it was vague. One thing he seemed sure of is that Smiley had told him he was inside his head.

When he was done Caleb let Rusty have the cigarettes though it cost him an effort of will to deliver on that promise. He left the interview room and found Tom leaning against the wall, empty handed. Hank stood off at the end of the corridor, watching them.

'Nothing?'

Tom shook his head.

'No footage of him in the emergency entrance to the surface. They've got cameras in the desert up to a mile out from the facility and none of them show anything though we thought him trying to surface was a slim shot anyway. All cargo is routinely searched and accounted for and the records look good, so he probably didn't stowaway. He would have been caught at the other end at one of the colonies anyway. It's like he up and disappeared.'

'You're starting to sound like Mr Inattentive over there,' Caleb muttered.

Tom sniggered and Caleb chuckled with him.

'What's next?' Tom said.

'Not sure.' Caleb bit his lip. 'We're missing something.'

'You figured it out yet?' Hank called. The tone of his voice suggested he thought it highly unlikely. Caleb wondered how someone could ping-pong between self pity and mindless arrogance so quickly.

'Working on it,' Caleb said.

Hank nodded.

'Well, if you won't be needing anything else. I'll escort you to your quarters.'

Hank led them out of the metal bee-hive of the staff rooms and across the docking bay. The docking bay must have been nearly half a mile across. Freight ships sat like sleeping swans every few hundred feet, their burnished metal gleaming. Unlike junkers they only had serial numbers written on their sides to denote them.

As they crossed the bay Hank talked to himself, or rather, to the air in general.

'I apologise if these quarters are more cramped than the ones you had before. We're moving things around a little.' Caleb paused. He looked up at the blast doors overhead like a tremendous lid. He wondered if this is what a wasp felt like being shut inside a jam jar.

'This is where he would have fallen.'

'That's right,' Hank said. 'Searched the whole area and couldn't find anything. Every room. Staff quarters. Every ship was grounded for days. Nothing.'

Caleb spun slowly on the spot, in his mind he tried to recreate the scene like an artist imposing an imagined image onto a real landscape. He visualised Smiley rising, perhaps clutching at an injured leg. He saw him taking stock of his surroundings, the way a soldier would, scanning for cover points. As he spun he saw the door from which they'd just come leading to the staff area. Though Smiley was familiar with it from all the times he'd been interviewed he wouldn't have gone down there: far too many personnel and a dead end. Caleb kept turning. The far door for the guest quarters was similarly a dead end. Nothing there. He would have looked at the ships and known he had no chance to getting on board.

The only solution was he would have run across the bay.

Caleb started walking.

Tom leapt after him. Hank limped behind.

'What're you doing?' he croaked.

'This is the only way he could have gone.'

'Ain't nothing up there.'

'We'll see.'

Caleb had become sure in the same way he was sure in a dream that something was waiting for him at the other end of the bay.

When they reached the other side they were faced with a blast door significantly more imposing than any of the other security doors in the building. Two guards winged the entrance.

'This wasn't here last time we were here,' Tom said, giving Hank a murderous look.

'Like I said, we were building a solitary confinement wing between level 12 and the docking bay for people like Smiley. If he'd been locked up in there he would never have gotten out.'

Caleb fought down the urge to scream and throw Hank on the floor and stamp on his injured leg until it cracked. He was on the verge of something, he could feel it like the urgent moment before a dream startles into wakefulness. He had to think.

'What did this look like four months ago? When Smiley was here.'

'Just a dirty hole in the wall. They were still digging.'

Caleb felt his heart begin to pump as though he'd been given a shot of adrenaline. Colours were starting to grow warmer. He felt high.

'And you forgot to fucking mention it?' Tom roared. He spat on the floor and turned away. 'Un-fucking-believable.' He rounded on the warden. 'We said no fucking bullshitting Hank! No fucking bullshitting!'

Two black circles had appeared under Hank's armpits and his brow glistened.

'Look,' he said, holding up his hands. 'Mars's crust is full of tunnels like an ant's nest. But it's treacherous. Building is a nightmare. We did look down there for him but...' Hank whimpered. 'He's probably fallen down one of those endless holes. He's a gonner.'

'And what if one of these tunnels led to the surface, Hank? Outside the range of the fucking cameras you've got set up.'

Hank was shaking as though he was about to have a fit. He swayed on his bad leg.

'There's no way he could have survived down there! No water. No food. Limited oxygen. He's dead. You two just need to accept that!' Hank took a shuddering breath. He was bright red. 'Now I have to escort you to your quarters.'

Tom and Caleb shared a dark look and followed him without a word. When they sat in the squat room alone, Tom turned to Caleb.

'This is a fuck up on a legendary scale, Cal.'

Caleb nodded and lay down on his bed, hands clasped over his chest.

'Do you think he could have survived?'

Caleb thought about it a while.

'He survived a nuclear war, Tom. I think he could survive just about anything.'

<>ACCESS LOGS</>
   <>MARS CONTAINMENT FACILITY 006</>
   <>RECORD NO. 101009</>
   <>CREATED 09:00:45 28/12/2060 EARTH TIME</>
   <>BEGIN RECORD</>

IT IS NOT HUMAN INGENUITY, but the influence of the gods that has spawned all art, all advancement, all literature, all music. This is why when a poet finishes a masterpiece they say they feel as if someone else wrote it. The Greeks were correct in assuming there was a muse, but the way they interpreted the divine muse was mistaken, and they missed the *purpose.* All true art serves a purpose. It is not art for art's sake – to massage the ego of the artist or to expound some phony political ideology. It is an illustration of divine order.

The lie of art is the very truth. And that is who the Masked God is. He is the lie that tells the truth.

When you try to pull off his mask, you will find it is not a mask.

But it is not a face, either.

<>RECORD SUSPENDED</>

Day 3

28TH DECEMBER 2068

He had walked in absolute darkness for two days without rest and without water. There was nothing except the bleak tunnel before him. Sometimes he realised he could not feel his feet and he felt as if he floated as in his dreams, drawn through a liquid black portal. Other times the pain resurged and the caves would swallow his screams.

There was a promise of another world on the other side of this darkness, a world in which the godheads breathed. If he could only reach it he knew he could be saved. He had been told about this world long ago, in the years after the war, in the years of hollowness and white rooms and medicine. 2046, he'd been admitted to the psychiatric ward and Smiley knew that they intended to keep him there forever. Underneath the catatonia his mind had run on like a hibernating computer program. They intended to medicate him. Lobotomise him in slow degrees with scalpels of the mind that cut too fine to see the wound. But he'd had no way out. No hopeful thought.

It wasn't exactly *what* he'd seen in the war, but rather, that he'd seen *behind.* He had seen the naked ugliness that lay beneath every smiling face, the knitted red tissue staring with death's eternal grin. He'd seen that behind Jack Fender's courage, there was only the bare instinct for survival. Behind that instinct there was nothing. He was not a courageous soldier: he was a pleading animal scrabbling at a wall to seize momentary freedom. It sickened Smiley so deeply to think of his death, so ignominious, so pathetic.

But as he'd sat in his wheelchair in the harsh empty white hospital ward he'd seen a woman hunched over in an old chair in the shadows, away from the others. It seemed to him that the only colour in the whole room lived inside the shadow that fell in the corner of the room and in the face of this woman. She beckoned with a single slender finger and he stood from his wheelchair and walked over to where she sat and knelt by her. She'd looked young, perhaps even beautiful, and yet streaks of white like rushing stars discoloured her tawny hair. The true age however was in her eyes: the eyes of someone who has watched a planet turn suspended in deep space. He saw the cosmos in her gaze.

She leant towards him, slow and fragile. Her bones were weak. Only living too long outside of gravity could make bones that weak. But something lived in her that did not live in any of the others in the ward.

'Who are you?'

'I am master,' she said, with a certainty that chilled him, that made his hair stand on end. 'And you are the pupil.'

'Yes,' he said. 'What will you teach me?'

'I will teach you how to pull off the mask and see there is no mask,' she croaked. Her eyes had begun to glow like embers breathed upon in the hushed darkness. 'I will teach you how to open and close the jaws of the mouth inside you. I will teach you how to fall along the strands of the great web. Many things. But most importantly, I will teach you how to *see.*'

'How to see?'

She'd nodded.

'Even when there is nothing to see. You will see.'

Craig Smiley thought of that now in the utter darkness that seemed to press and fold and close around him like a liquid. He needed to see, to see through.

He stumbled and went down onto his hands and knees. Breathing was becoming difficult. The oxygen gauge that flashed across his helmet visor showed he had barely 4% of his tank left. Soon he would run out of air and then it would be over. All his work in this world snapped off in a blip. Perhaps it would be better that way? Perhaps in death he would see the gods he'd sought so long in life.

But what if he'd failed them?

He crawled along in the blackness.

There was some last secret the old prophetess had not shared. He'd done everything and yet the gateway had never opened. Seven sacrifices to seven gods. Seven years in prison. Seven... Seven...

He felt along with his hands. His finger brushed a stone and he moved it aside. He pulled himself along. He felt like an animal carrying the weight of the planet on his back. He could hardly draw air. Though the darkness showed nothing it started to swarm as if with microcosmic life, living atoms. Perplexing colour danced.

He crawled on. It was only now he considered the persistent ache in his chest might be his heart beating against all odds. Suddenly, looming out of the darkness he saw the corpse of his father lying there like a discarded toy.

'Just remember son,' the corpse said. 'Selling is never about the product, it's about making the customer *like you*. That way, they *want* to buy. Neat trick, eh?'

Smiley screamed. This was not a howl of pain. This was frustration curdled into sound, a scream that sought to cut out of the circularity of life. He knew he was hallucinating from the lack of oxygen, but of all the things it would be possible to see his father and his deluded materialism brought him least comfort.

He swiped at the vision and his hand passed through nothing. Again there was only darkness. He forced himself on. The gauge dropped to 2%. He was going to die. He was going to fail. Her, them, himself. Everything. His hand slipped on the stone and he fell down flat on his face; the hand found emptiness and he realised he was no longer in a tunnel but crawling along the narrow top of some precipice. He shifted his body until his head hovered over the lip and he looked down and could see no bottom.

The gauge dropped to 1%. He heard his breaths as rattling as those of an old, asthmatic man. He felt his heart weak and faltering. He had nothing left. No plan. No escape. He had only one thing more that he could do: cast himself into that emptiness. It would be better than dying like a beaten pack animal.

He rolled, slowly, a growl coming to his throat. Even in the low gravity his weight felt like the leaden cloak of the traitors in Dante's hell. His growl became a scream, but then he pushed and was flung onto his back and over the edge. He fell and felt as though he was falling in slow motion. All was soundless – he was a stone dropping into a black pool of such magnitude his ripples could not disturb the surface.

His back cracked on something hard and he cried out and flipped over so he tumbled face first. He had a sense of elation, of euphoric joy as though he'd taken flight. Then the darkness became solid. He saw no floor. It was as though an invisible hand reached out of the abyss and caught him. The impact crushed his chest, his lungs, and pain sprouted like a bamboo shoot up through his leg. The visor of his helmet smashed in a shrieking spatter of glass and he yelled as the shards drove into his face.

And in that moment he realised there was atmosphere.

He breathed.

For minutes he lay there, still, at the bottom of the pit. The air tasted like iron-heavy water drunk from an old spring. Then he pulled off the ruin of his helmet and pushed himself up to his knees, trembling.

And there it was.

It shone with clarity so perfect that all his memories and dreams seemed like insubstantial light from a dull bulb compared to rays from the sun. The cavern was illuminated and around him, graven into the walls, were images of the deities of whom he'd dreamed for twenty years. He could not begin to imagine who or what had scratched these images into the rock and at what distant epoch in the life of Mars. They were ancient – that much was certain. Sitting at the centre of the room was something disturbingly modern. It was an astronaut's helmet and on it were printed the initials S.P. Anyone else might have wondered why the helmet had been abandoned here but not Craig Smiley. He knew *exactly* why.

She had been here. His master had knelt exactly where he knelt. And now he would become master too.

The vision intensified like a fever. The silver outline of a door shimmered as though submerged. As he watched the vision swelled and grew until it became a nebulous cloud that enveloped him and he was *part* of the vision, not merely observing it.

At last he was through the door.

And on the other side he saw a glimpse of what he had struggled his whole life to see. Theologians and philosophers and writers of the ages had called it many names: Hades, Tuonela, Duat, Heaven. Even Carcosa. There were shades of them all and yet it was like none.

The cavern was lit by a sun that was not a sun but a glowering lidded eye opening. A pain like a needle seared through Craig Smiley's forehead, through the pineal gland, the "third eye". He felt the walls of the cavern slough away into nothingness. The eye regarded him, vast beyond imagining and brighter than a star.

There were other forms in the deep. And in fact, the deep itself was a *form:* circular and cavernous. At its heart was a deeper darkness from which spewed endless streams of cosmic light and matter. Looking into that darkness pained Smiley because what lay behind it was beyond even his thought.

Other, smaller figures filled the cosmic space. A spider curled itself over a barren rock and impregnated it with a thousand, thousand eggs. A god with a single, gigantic horn pierced the surface of a planet and made it split. It drank the magma from its core and Smiley shook with something between fear and ecstasy.

All of a sudden he dropped, stars and cracked worlds streaming past him too numerous to count and blurred into streaks of orange and white light. He plummeted faster than he'd fallen over the lip of the precipice and landed weightlessly on the surface of a dune-ridden world. He saw his teacher there standing quietly by an empty wheelchair. He walked towards her and she smiled. She pointed at the chair.

'This is for you,' she said.

Smiley sat down slowly. She began to wheel him over the sands. Ahead he saw there was a darkened hut. His heart beat hard in his chest when he saw that hut and he had the sensation of having seen it before in his childhood though he knew it couldn't be as he'd grown up in the city. He looked to his teacher and her face was rigid as a mask, staring ahead at the hut. He tried to rise from the chair but couldn't, he was transfixed.

Slowly, the door to the darkened hut swung open.

A figure appeared at the doorway and Smiley's whole body felt as though filled with an electrical charge. He writhed in his chair. He could hardly look at it. The figure was frighteningly human and yet inhuman. Unlike the cosmic beings that had filled up the universe this being had the arms and legs and head of a person, but it was thin, impossibly thin like an image of death. It was naked and sexless and a crown of broken glass circled its head. Smiley knew without asking it was a King. *The King.*

Craig Smiley. It said without speaking. *You have travelled a long way. We have watched you with great pleasure. Your work is pleasing, but unfinished.*

'The gateway never opened,' he whispered.

The King tilted his head.

Did it not? If you had not made those offerings, you would never have come to Mars. You would never have escaped the facility. You would not be here now.

Like a slow sunrise, light which was also pulsing energy swept up Smiley from his toes to his temples. He was half delirious.

'Then it was all...it all meant...'

The King nodded.

But there is more to do. The gate in your mind has been opened. But there is another gate.

The King pointed upwards. In the sky above them the Mouth spun like a suspended, flat disc, churning and regurgitating in endless cycle. Its cavernous maw was space itself and inside the space was a throat of absolute blackness. Now Smiley looked at it again he knew it was a portal though he still could not begin to wrap his mind around its depths or measures as though it existed in a fourth dimension of shape he could not quantify.

If we are to heal your broken world, the Black Gate must be opened.

The word 'heal' was like honey on the lips of someone famished –

ambrosia for the starved Apollo. Smiley drank it in. Heal. That was what he wanted. The broken, barren, sightless world to be healed. That was why he had called on the gods. That was why he had done all those things which some said were terrible.

The King put a hand on Smiley's shoulder and smiled a smile that filled him with the dread of the universe.

One more offering is required. These caves will tell you where it must be done.

'What caves?'

But the vision was already slipping. He felt as though a hook had attached to his spine and hoisted him out of the chair and away from the strange little hut and the red sands. The constellations spun around him forming a whirlwind tunnel of light.

Then he was alone in a dark cavern and everything was silent. Craig Smiley: convict, killer, madman, put his bleeding face in his hands and wept. Like a child robbed of a mother, he wept.

He reached out and put his hands on the helmet which lay there still in the darkness and felt along the side. Eventually he found a small bump and flipped a small switch. A torch-light flickered into being illuminating the space around him.

It was the time for action. He had been on the verge of despair and death but now he'd been resurrected. He needed to get out of the caves and into one of the mining colonies. To do that, he'd have to hide his face. He had no doubt it was already on every screen on the planet. He looked at the blacked-out visor of the old helmet and searched his reflection.

Thick stubble was already sprouting across his chin, upper lip and neck, making his face look fuller and more homely. Meanwhile the scars from the glass had rendered his nose twisted and unrecognisable. The skin around the sockets of his eyes was distorted. The cuts in his cheeks lengthened his face.

He laughed. He was wearing a mask that was no mask.

He picked up the helmet and placed it over his head. It was an old 2K30 model from the original human explorations of Mars, but it fit the body armour well enough. There was a small sub-oxygen tank attached which he reckoned could probably top up his own by at least 10% -

enough to make it back to o-six. He was sure that this one chamber was the only place in these tunnels with any atmosphere. He did not doubt for a second he would know the way back to the facility.

He adjusted the angle of the light and peered closely at the strange hieroglyphic art on the walls. It showed crude depictions of the seven gods he recognised but all of them were connected by a dark web-like star, much like the one he had drawn on the window two days ago when he first escaped. This one, however, was far more detailed and complex and at its heart, instead of a black spot, there was a door shining with some unknowably coloured light. Printed on this door were numbers that could only be coordinates. Smiley performed a visual capture using the helmet's camera.

Slowly, he stood and turned to look at the sheer, harsh face of rock. He had not eaten or drunk water for two days but he did not need to because his soul had been fed on manna that would last him a lifetime.

With a grin to match even the King's, he climbed out of the pit.

<>ACCESS LOGS</>
    <>PSYCHOLOGICAL   CLINIC   AUSTIN   POLICE   DEP.
TEXAS EARTH</>
    <>RECORD NO. 658</>
    <>CREATED 08:30:00 22/10/2058 EARTH TIME</>
    <>BEGIN RECORD</>

I've been doing a lot of reading to try and come to terms with this religion of his. I think this is the key to figuring out what he's doing. But it's not simple. It's not anything I can find anywhere else. It's like it all comes from his head. Maybe it does...

But then, there are echoes of every kind of myth and legend in it. The girl he burned resembles the Greek story of Semele, for example. Semele asked Zeus to show himself in his true form and she was incinerated just by looking at him.

Then there's Louise. He pulled her stomach out through her damn mouth. He painted the words on her corpse: "From the Mouth of Nothing Flows Milk and Blood". In ancient Greek theology Chaos was the first and oldest god: a dark gaping space. But he gave birth to Gaia, mother earth, and Eros, the god of sexual desire. Gaia is often typified as a fertile breast-feeding matriarch. Eros is the hot-blooded lover. Maybe he's trying to say something, make some statement through universal symbols? I don't know.

What do you mean I'm too involved? This is my fucking job.

I know I'm not supposed to talk about the case here but fuck the protocol. Would you rather I didn't think about it? Sank a few beers and got drunk on the weekends like Tom and the rest of those selfish bastards?

He's still out there, dammit.

He's still fucking out there.

<>RECORD SUSPENDED</>

DAY 41

Eleanor walked the deck of the *Penelope* and checked every bolt was in place and every door lock mechanism worked and every pipe and wire was secure. It wasn't that she didn't trust her ship. On the contrary, she trusted it more than anyone else she could name, even Jim. In space, one bolt or one screw could mean the end of everything.

The night previous she'd made use of Mars's dayless, nightless hours. She'd told Hank to meet her on the *Penelope* at 12:00 ready to leave Mars. After Hank had left the Rock Biter, she and Jim had gone down to the Red Devil and spoken with an old contact who was a dab hand at electronically forging freight papers. In the eyes of the law she had now been made the official custodian of an emergency shipment of produce up to the Dome, another colony some 160 miles east towards the mountains.

Eleanor liked to think of the deck as the glue that held the ship together. A blast door near the ship's rear on the portside formed the exit. Four doors set equidistant along the corridor allowed access to the cramped rooms that formed the quarters for crew and passengers alike.

At one end of the deck a secured door led to the pilot room and at the other the engine room which was too hot to enter during take-off. A hatch connecting to a narrow shaft running through the ship's under-belly allowed access to wiring and also panels that controlled life-support modules.

She swiped her security card on the reader by the pilot room door and entered. Unlike most junkers the nose of *Penelope* was overlarge, rather like her own nose Eleanor often thought, which allowed room for an extra circular table behind the pilot's seats (screwed into the floor) on which her and Jim had played countless games of cards. These games were played on touchscreens, else the cards would get lost in zero gravity.

'You still want to go through?' Jim said, swivelling in the second's seat and fixing an intense stare on her.

'Yes,' she said, weary. 'I'd have thought breaking the law in order to do good would have been right up your street?'

Jim bit his lip and said nothing.

At 12:03 someone buzzed to enter the ship and Eleanor looked down at the screens on her dashboard which showed the view from the miniature camera feed in the junker door. She saw the scarred, ugly face of the prison warden. She opened the door for him and went out to meet him on deck.

It was only standing inside her junker that she realised he was a big man. Certainly not fat, given the way his combat armour hugged his body. She wondered whether there was anything between his skin and his bone. He carried with him a presence that extended outwards around him. It didn't help a heavy calibre weapon was slung over his back. It was the kind of weapon that could clear out a bar the size of the Rock Biter in one sweep.

'What's that for?'

'In case he resists arrest,' Hank said. There was something soft in his eyes which contrasted starkly with the hard, grimness of the face. He glanced around and smiled. Jim hovered in the doorway to the pilot's room like a sceptred shadow, but Hank seemed not to notice or else to care. 'This is a nice ship,' he said. 'Is it named after the wife of Odysseus?'

Eleanor's mouth almost dropped open. She knew back on Earth there were plenty of people who'd read *The Odyssey* or else vaguely knew its premise. It was, after all, a famous legend, one that'd survived long enough to prove its merit. But she had not expected to find someone out here other than herself or Jim who'd cotton on and still less a prison warden. There was something resembling the very solid, earthen ores and minerals they handled about the colony workers. Art seemed to have little place in the hearts of those who'd chosen to live on Mars and for those in whom it did have a place they kept it to themselves.

Hank was smiling.

'Some say that Penelope is a cipher for Odysseus's own soul.' He reached out and touched the metal wall as though the cheek of a newborn babe. 'Do you wish your soul could take flight, Captain Cole?'

She stood, speechless, watching him. No one had ever talked to her like that, not even Jim. Jim was full of philosophical ideas but he did not use them to read a heart's hidden writing.

Eventually, she gathered herself. Fine sentiments were one thing, but she had to remember her other reasons for doing this.

'I trust you are ready to make the down-payment?'

'Shouldn't we get into the air first?' he tried a winning smile which was lost beneath his scraggly facial hair. 'How do I know you won't take my money and then tell me to go my way?'

The feeling that'd washed over her when he talked about *Penelope* ebbed.

'How do I know once we're in the air and unable to turn around that you won't refuse what we agreed?' she said, bringing the kind of firmness a manager of a global corporation would envy into her voice.

Hank held up his hands and shrugged.

'You win.'

She led him through the pilot room where the three of them sat down around the table and she swept her hand across the touchscreen a few times until it brought up her accounts page. Hank was taking stock of his surroundings, like a wild animal introduced to a new environment. His eyes flitted over every instrument, button and crevice of the room as though suspicious of them or as if he was trying to memorise where they lay. That made Eleanor nervous.

'20,000, as agreed?' she said, unable to stop her lips from tightening. She would not believe any of what he'd said until that 20,000 hit her account.

Hank nodded and drew out his card. She did her own check and swiftly read the name initialised on the card. It said: HANK A. MARSHALL, just as it should. He placed it on the touchscreen face up and a prompt flashed up.

BEGIN TRANSFER? Y/N

'Yes,' she said.

It prompted for the amount.

'Twenty thousand credits,' Hank said. He sat very differently to how he had at the Rock Biter. He was hunched over, shoulders slumped. He had a look of dejection that reminded Eleanor of when she was facing an irksome task the next day, like arse-kissing at one of her annual reviews so they didn't revoke her junker license. Hank's dejection was on another scale though: he looked like someone told they're terminal. She told herself anyone would look like that losing so much money. He was probably having second thoughts about his initial offer, wishing he'd haggled.

A load screen appeared along with a buffering circle. Eleanor realised she was actually sweating. Jim's fingers never left the wolf's head of his cane.

Then a message flashed up in unmistakable red letters.

TRANSACTION DECLINED. CARD CLOSED. REPLACE-MENT CARD HAS BEEN ISSUED TO CARDHOLDER.

Eleanor looked up at Hank.

He sighed deeply.

'I thought that might happen.'

Eleanor did not truly see Hank move. One minute he was sitting, half slumped opposite her. The next he was behind her and something thin and cold pressed against her neck; his fingers were laced through her hair pulling back her head. Jim was on his feet, the wolf's head handle un-notched revealing six inches of the concealed, fine blade inside the cane.

Eleanor struggled to breathe. Next to her, Hank panted like a rabid dog in her ear.

'I tried to play nice,' he said. 'I didn't want to have to do it this way, but you leave me no choice.'

Jim's hand was white on the sword-cane. He looked as though he'd been turned to stone. She knew he wouldn't dare do anything while she was hostage.

'You bastard.'

Hank laughed.

'Oh I'm much, much worse than a bastard, Captain Cole. My father was a *bastard*: he cared more about himself than anyone I've ever known.' He pressed the blade harder into her neck so it nicked the skin. A warm bead of liquid trickled down like a slow worm. 'I'm Charybdis. Stray too close and...' He whistled, making a sound like something falling into a deep well.

Jim slid the sword slowly back into the cane and set it to lean against the table. The azure in his eyes burned like biting ice. Hank, or whatever his real name was, hoisted Eleanor up to her feet. He was strong, freakishly so for a man so thin, and the blade on her neck was steady. She had no doubt he could sever her windpipe with a flick of his wrist.

'What do you want me to do?' Jim said, quietly.

Hank laughed again.

'I'm so relieved you skipped the boring part about asking me to let her go! It's simple. I want you to pilot this ship out of here. Do what I say and neither of you has to die.'

Jim nodded and went to take his cane. Hank pulled on Eleanor's hair and toyed with the knife against her skin. Jim withdrew his hand and walked slowly over to the console and sat down. Even shaking and scared shitless she had to admire Jim for the way he sat down at that console. He had dignity in everything he did.

'Good,' Hank said.

Jim's fingers skirted across the controls and in a few seconds the *Penelope* rattled and the thrusters roared like an earthquake. The ship detached from the ground and drew in its landing gear and floated up through the dock. The man who had pretended to be Hank Marshall dragged Eleanor over to the other pilot chair and forced her to sit down. His eyes were on Jim and the bay window through which they could see the dock falling away like a final zoom-out in a film, but she knew he was still alert.

After a few minutes a warning light flashed on to tell them an obstruction approached the top of the junker. Moments later a clinical female voice droned out of the intercom.

'Thank you for your trade at the Iron Caves...' It spoke with that strange absence of rhythm common to automated voices. It was only when you heard speech without music that you realised just how much like music it was. '...I hope you had a pleasant stay. Please confirm whether your destination is Mars-internal or interplanetary.'

'Mars-internal,' Jim said, without hesitation.

'Good boy,' Hank whispered.

'Thank you. Please confirm your destination and shipping reference.'

'The Dome. 35558.'

There was a pause where Eleanor prayed for the first time in her life that the forgery had been a botch job and they got caught. She knew her man and they had dealt together for years but a part of her still hoped that he'd fucked up. She told herself no one got it right all the time. This could be that time. The woman's voice returned with an uplifting series of beeps which made Eleanor feel like vomiting. She swallowed and felt as though she might choke.

'Priority shipment status confirmed. Have a pleasant journey.'

There was a bright flash and then a nasal klaxon rang out throughout the entire colony like an old war siren. The sound of an immense mechanism juddering into motion drowned out all else except the psychotic breathing in her ear.

Starlight washed down on them, ephemeral, like a memory returning half formed in a dream. The ship rose like a night-bird into a star-spangled sky without cloud and Eleanor remembered summer nights on Earth on the coasts and her heart ached like an old woman's for previous times. She did not know quite what had brought it on: whether it was the fear of death or the sight of the stars after so long cooped up in the colony, but the ache would not dull for any rational thought. The light poured through the glass and she thought about how she used to lie on the beach stargazing: she thought about the *beauty* of the light and the poetry in it. She wondered how many years that light had taken to reach them and over what seemingly unlimited expanse of darkness it had passed.

And in contemplating the light she wondered where her own path would now lead, over what darkness, and whose startled gaze it would reach out in the dimness.

'There are mag-boots in that unit,' Jim said, nodding at the metal storage unit fixed to the wall. His voice was so quiet that even against the nothing-backdrop of space Eleanor barely heard him. Jim had fixed her with his shining blue eyes as he spoke and she felt as though something had been meant by that look but she couldn't grasp it.

Her captor glanced over his shoulder to check the storage unit and nodded.

'We're going to take this real slow,' he said.

He let go of Eleanor's hair and swung the machine gun round with the freed hand whilst still keeping the knife firmly against her neck. She considered throwing herself backwards and trying to knock him to the ground or else head-butting him but she caught Jim's eye and she thought she saw the faintest shake of the head. He was right. Still too vulnerable. *If only there was a way she could upset his balance.*

Then it hit her. The opportunity was moments away from occurring. There would be a few seconds as they entered zero-g that he would be disorientated. As a prisoner, he'd probably never been off-planet in years. It would also take him a few seconds to strap on his mag-boots.

The knife slid away from Eleanor's throat like the tendril of some many-limbed monster and she found that up until now she'd practically been holding her breath. She turned in her seat and came nose to nose with the wide-nozzled barrel of a gun.

'Nice and easy now,' he said, as though coaxing an animal into a cage. 'I want you to go over to the unit and take out the boots and put them on me. No games or I blow a hole in his kneecap and then he'll need the cane.'

He smiled like a like a child entertainer as he said it: an ice-cream man or a clown. One children would later look back on with deep unease.

Eleanor stood and walked slowly to the unit. Already she could feel gravity lessening as the planet let go of them. If she took her time...

'Come on,' he snapped. He aimed the gun at Jim's knee and she hurried. She opened the metal cabinet and took out one of three pairs of mag-boots.

'Put on yours and his and put mine on the floor.'

She quickly attached her own and then threw a second pair to Jim who put them on while sitting down. Finally she put the third pair down at his feet. He stepped into them.

'Strap them in place.'

Eleanor bent down to the boots. Her stomach started to feel like it had detached from the rest of her gut and floated around her body. It was a familiar sensation – a kind of nausea that accompanied gravity lowering, but with that was something else: the feeling that as the cord collaring them to Mars thinned inch by inch so too did the cord to all sanity. Anything could happen out in the great dark.

She strapped the first boot tight as she could. Her hands trembled as she worked. The whole time she watched the inmate's eyes which moved between her and Jim like one of the three locked in a stand-off at the end of *The Good, The Bad, and The Ugly*. Her stomach gave another lurch. They were moments away from zero g.

She decided to do something crazy.

She waited a precious half second for his eyes to shift from her and then dropped her shoulder and threw herself forward in a rugby tackle. She caught the inmate round the midriff and he stumbled backwards. Jim rose from the controls and ran for his cane. The ship bucked and dropped to one side. Both she and the prisoner went slamming against the wall and Jim's cane rolled away from him across the floor.

Eleanor held on as though to a precipice overlooking a bottomless pit. She knew if he twisted free from her she wouldn't stand a chance. Her head was blood-heavy and her arms felt like they would break if she gripped any harder. A hand reached up under her throat and *squeezed*. She choked and her grip was broken. The hand was strong as a monster's in a nightmare. It lifted her and threw her against the wall as though she was a fish he'd snared only to discard back into the waters. The impact crushed the air out of her lungs but the pain didn't end there. There was a momentary flash as she saw a glinting metal gun-butt and then she was face down on the floor spitting out two teeth. The cord she'd imagined tethering her to sanity and grounding snapped and it was as if she'd been cast out into space, spinning uncontrollably. For the first time she became afraid of space, afraid of travelling through the darkness without anything to hold her or stop her spinning. All she wanted was to plant her feet on earth's sure surface and forget she ever dreamed of going out into the darkness alone because out on the edge of things there were men like the one on their ship now who weren't men but something else incarnated from all natal fear. Everything grew dim. The taste of blood seemed to transmute into more than taste and overcome her whole body like a slow coldness.

Distantly, she heard a gunshot. Jim screamed and his body hit the floor with a sound like meat being slapped onto a counter. That was the last thing before she blacked out.

<>ACCESS LOGS</>
    <>AUSTIN POLICE DEP. TEXAS EARTH</>
    <>EXHIBIT NO. 7</>
    <>EXHIBIT FOUND ON SUSPECT'S PERSON AT POINT OF ARREST</>
    <>BEGIN RECORD</>

there are those who will not see
they walk as blind-men walk
insensible to sound or thought
their tongueless lips emit a dying plea

but those who see and those who dream
these are the truly cursed
like open cuts they bleed and in the seam
pours all shame and every sin
the universe

<>RECORD TERMINATES</>

DAY 121

Caleb lay on the bed of his guest room and stared at the whitewashed ceiling, chewing nicotine gum. He was starting to think that maybe Hank was right. Maybe Craig Smiley had gone into the caves because he was a fox hemmed in by wolves and then gotten lost and died there. He was human, after all, for all his talk of gods.

But somehow that just didn't sit right with him. It was like the ending to *1984*, a book his dad had made him read half a dozen times as a kid. Caleb often wondered how his dad could *like* that book. It was interesting, vivid certainly, and the language was well composed, but how could anyone be satisfied with an ending like that? He knew it was meant to make a point but that didn't change the fact it left him hollow.

That's how Caleb felt about his own life. Sure, he could have gotten shot right through the heart or died in a car chase. He could have had his guts spilled on the streets or his head caved in a dozen times or more. But if life was a book and God was its author, he wasn't meant to die that way. He was meant to have an ending. A proper one. He wasn't sure whether it was faith or arrogance, but it'd worked for him so far.

Deep down he felt the same way about Smiley although there was a difference in that Smiley was the villain of the story and the reason he was not meant to die rotting in a cave somewhere was that Caleb was meant to catch him.

But a detective couldn't base a case on hunches. Tom had said from the start finding a body was unlikely with such a delay in coming to the investigation. He stood up and spat out his gum into a rubbish bin. He shouldn't lie there all day. He'd visit the staff bar. Talk to a few more guards. Maybe one of them would say something. That's all you needed sometimes. Just somebody to say something.

Caleb had been able to tell from Hank Marshall's weight and breath that he was a heavy drinker but what he saw in the Staff Common Room was something else. It reminded him just how near to insane all people were, how underneath their vestments of work and their smiles and their government approved credit there was a hunched, snarling creature that lived to fill its belly and alleviate the pain of years with every substance or thrill it could find. A person who lost all principles was baser than any animal.

The top three buttons of his shirt were undone revealing oily chest hair turning grey at the tips. His cheeks and the skin under his eyes drooped as though swollen with the liquor he'd poured into his body. Ten empty shot glasses stood in a trail along the bar and he cradled an eleventh in his hand like an injured bird he would nurse back to health once sober enough. In his other hand he held his credit card. Under the crimson light of the bar his skin looked yellowing.

Caleb sat down next to Hank and ordered a beer.

'You look beat,' he said.

'Come to arrest me, detective?'

'I told you. Only one person I'm lookin' to arrest.'

Hank snorted and finished his whiskey.

'Another.'

The barman nodded and held out a terminal. Hank placed his card on the reader and it beeped in approval. Caleb wondered whether Hank intended to keep doing that until a message flashed up telling him he'd emptied his entire bank balance and was at last completely finished.

The barman put down a beer in front of him. Caleb paid and took a sip. The hit was instant. Rich, cold, bitterer than the beer he was used to on Earth but with dryness like something salty he wanted to taste again.

'Do you think you will catch him?' Hank murmured. He turned unfocused eyes on Caleb. He looked like a side-character that'd gotten bitten in a zombie movie and was just about to turn

'I know we will,' he said.

Hank laughed quietly.

'You detectives are always so damn sure of everything.' He turned his eyes back on the amber liquid in his glass and drank. 'Shame it doesn't work for your personal life ain't it?'

He finished the shot and slammed it down. He twisted on his stool and leant forward, washing Caleb with the smell of alcohol. Caleb saw where this was going. He leapt off his stool and grabbed Hank's shirt; he twisted his hands and feet together and slammed the warden up against the bar. The shot glasses went flying and Caleb clocked that other off duty guards had stood up.

'Steady, Hank. Steady.'

He gave an apologetic look around at the others and one of the off duty guards cracked a lame joke about Hank 'marshalling' himself and the room settled. The bartender swept up the glass and Caleb forced Hank into a seat. He was wheezing. He didn't seem to realise what just happened.

'My personal life is just that,' Caleb whispered. 'Personal.'

Hank stared at him like a beaten gladiator awaiting the sentence of the emperor.

'You...' He swallowed and held out a hand to catch the barman's attention.

'He's had enough,' Caleb said, meeting the bartender's eye. He nodded and ignored Hank's waving hand. The warden slumped down over the bar, limp and pathetic. Caleb couldn't help but think of an unerect cock.

'You know,' Hank slurred. 'They used to have girls here. Dancers...' He flapped his hand in the direction of the rest of the bar. 'Frank thought it was good for morale and man he was right. No chance of getting any of that action under the Bitch. Got to go all the way to the fucking Iron Caves...' He tried to gesture for the bartender again. When the bartender ignored him he swore obscenely.

'You go outside the facility?'

'Yeah. Can't spend our whole lives cooped up in here all the time. We'd go stir-crazy. Even the Bitch knows that.'

Caleb nodded. It seemed so obvious but he'd never thought of it before. He supposed he'd imagined the staff taking leave and going back to Earth as opposed to elsewhere on Mars. He frowned. Something was niggling at him. Hank took regular trips to the Iron Caves for women. That must mean he and the other guards and wardens had a deal with the freight pilots. Presumably Carla Bolton knew about this but was turning a blind eye because as Hank said the guards needed it for morale.

Shit.

He reached inside his coat pocket and pulled out his touchscreen and pressed the shortcut key which dialled Tom's number. He picked up on the first ring.

'Tom, I've just had a hunch.'

'Shoot.'

He was sweating and his hand had started shaking. He felt like a coiled spring that was suddenly going to pop.

'What if Craig *did* leave by a freight ship?'

There was a hesitation.

'But Cal all the cargo was checked. Unless you're suggesting corruption...'

'I'm not. What if he didn't sneak on board? What if he wasn't in the cargo hold? What if he just *walked* on?'

'You're not making sense.'

'He was in a helmet,' Caleb plunged on, feeling like someone who'd been floating down a gentle river until now, when a deep undercurrent had taken him off down a new path. 'He was wearing body-armour and had Hank's old credit card. What if he spent a few days out in the caves then came out again and just walked right across the bay and got on a ship?'

Tom was silent for a few seconds. Then he whistled.

'I know daylight robbery is a thing Cal but I don't know whether he could pull that off.'

'It can't hurt to be sure,' Caleb said. 'We need to go to the Iron Caves.'

'I'll be down in twenty.'

Caleb looked up from the screen. Hank sat watching him, looking like someone who's seen their own death and cannot do anything to avoid it. He knew Hank expected him to say something but he had no words for him. If the warden wanted to drown in his own self pity and misery then he could. Caleb was done being dragged down with people. He stood and walked away from the bar.

'I did everything I damn well could,' Hank roared so loud everyone in the bar looked around. Caleb did not even turn.

'No you didn't,' he said, leaving.

An hour later he and Tom sat in the thrumming GC on their way to the Iron Caves. Tom was video-calling Melinda, explaining they were soon going to wrap things up, that everything was ok and that it was exactly as he'd thought. His face was lit by the crypt-like blue light of the touchscreen. The paleness it bestowed made him look sick. Caleb couldn't hear what she was saying because Tom had plugged in head-phones, but he almost thought he could lip-read Melinda's *come home soon* just before Tom swept his hand across the screen and it went dark.

'Everything alright?' Caleb said.

A muscle flexed in Tom's jaw. He re-attached the screen to its bracket on the wall and gave Caleb a look as though he'd asked him to do something despicable.

Caleb snorted and turned away from him. Try hard as he might he couldn't feel too sorry for Tom. It wasn't that he didn't know what it was like to miss someone. It wasn't even that he thought the job was more important than a family although he did. What bugged him was they were here now in the thick of it so there was no use wishing to be somewhere else. If Tom's mind wandered he was going to miss things and however intelligent Caleb was you always needed two pairs of eyes and two heads to crack a case.

'We have a job to do.'

'Don't you think I fucking know that Cal?'

Caleb forced himself to look Tom in the eye. He didn't like eyeballing people despite the fact Justin had once told him he had one of the most intense stares of anyone he'd ever met.

'I just want to get this guy.'

Tom huffed.

'And that's your fucking problem. This isn't about what really happened. You just couldn't live with the fact you didn't get him. Except you *did*, Cal. You got him first time when it counted. This is just a blip on the radar screen.'

Caleb paused. He had been sure of his own motives until just now. Maybe he was being selfish? Maybe it wasn't about Smiley and how dangerous he was at all – hell, he wouldn't be surprised if a few of the men he'd put away had escaped from their penitentiaries on earth. Maybe it was about him and his life and how if he wasn't doing this he was just another no-good detective on the brink of a crisis. Caleb didn't need to touch drugs or alcohol to be out of his mind, after all. All he needed were his dreams and the voices of little girls.

Tom grabbed the touchscreen from its bracket on the wall and set it down on his lap.

'What are you doing?'

Tom pulled a sour expression.

'*My job*. I'm checking the docking records.'

His finger skirted over the screen like the slender limb of a daddy-long-legs over the surface of a pond. After a while the finger paused.

'Two ships are recorded leaving the Iron Caves and not arriving at their specified destination the last three months,' Tom said. 'Junker 0829 "*Penelope*" and Junker 0993 "*Steel Tiger*".' He smirked at the latter's name. Caleb was more interested in the first. It was an odd name for a junker. '*Steel Tiger* hasn't got a clean record,' Tom said, scrolling onwards. 'Looks like it might be a good bet to start there.'

The docking headquarters was located at the very top of the colony just below the gigantic blast doors, aloof from the bars, taverns and secret clubs which made up the throbbing life of the Iron Caves. Caleb made a mental note to stop by the Rock Biter on their way out if their interview didn't go as planned. There were always loose tongues in places like that, and besides, it'd become something of a legend.

The headquarters itself was a squat round white disc. The side of it that faced out over the colony and docks was entirely transparent glass whilst the other side was flex-steel painted white. At the security door they were prompted to identify themselves and swipe their cards over a reader. It removed the need to introduce oneself – all their details were probably being examined on five or six screens manned by security personnel within. If they checked out they would be passed to someone with the authority to give them entry.

The door buzzed and slid open and they were met by a glamorous looking secretary.

'How can I help you?'

'We need to speak to the dock-master,' Tom said.

She pulled a face as though sympathising with an over-keen child.

'I'm sorry,' she said. 'But you'll have to take a seat in our waiting room. The dock-master is...'

'...very busy?' Tom growled. 'Yada Yada Yada. We hear that all the time. Normally we put up with it but today's different. Unless you and your boss want to be arrested for obstruction of justice you give us an audience right now.'

She swallowed. Caleb smiled on the inside. Tom probably had more grounds to arrest Caleb than he did this woman and the dock-master but she didn't have to know that.

'Right this way.'

They were led through a series of corridors not unlike the warren of Facility 006. The only different was that the "cells" were filled with smartly clad workers.

The first thing Caleb thought when they entered the dock-master's office was that the dock-master was a very different fish to his employees. He was chewing a raw lime and fiddling with a mechanical part on the table: Caleb wasn't great at machinery but he thought it might have been an exhaust valve. The dock-master's hands were filthy.

He put the lime in his mouth, wiped his hands on a cloth and then walked over and shook their hands and motioned for them to sit. If the secretary had reported to him about Tom's threat or if he was annoyed because he actually had said he was too busy to see them, he made no mention of either.

The dock-master caught Tom staring at the lime in his mouth.

'Got to keep your vitamin and mineral levels up,' he said, polishing off the last of the lime's skin and wiping his hands on his trousers, which was pointless given they were dirtied with the scum off the exhaust pipe. Caleb detected an accent that pointed to origins somewhere in the north of England. 'Wonderful irony this: we're here digging for minerals and yet we can't get none ourselves.' He smiled. 'Now, what can I do for you?'

His name was Peter Rouski and Caleb had the feeling that Peter was a man of eminent sense. Nothing he did or planned was ever without a practical purpose. He was not an outside-the-box thinker. He had done business for a long time in a certain way and it had proved successful and so he would keep doing business that way. The clothes of those around him might change. The ships might get glossier or better equipped. He would adapt without altering his essential nature. Caleb had respect for someone like that.

'Do you know where junker-0993 might have gotten to?'

Peter scratched his head.

'Name?'

'*Steel Tiger*,' Tom said.

'Ah,' he muttered. 'We sent out a few search droids for her once we failed to receive a confirmation it'd arrived at the Red Caves. Found what was left of her pretty quick. The captain of that junker - Nigel Quinlan - he never damn cleaned his ship. Paid for it in the end. Wiring got messed up and he lost control. He nose-dived into a rock.'

Peter sighed.

'What about the *Penelope*?' Caleb said. 'Set off around a similar time.'

'Never found her,' Peter said. Caleb thought he looked like a man who'd had a sudden great weight put on his shoulders. 'Terrible shame. Eleanor was a grand pilot. A little reckless sometimes, you know. But that's just her age. Cleaned her ship. Always paid her bills on time unlike some of them. Real good egg, you know.'

'It says on the logs she was headed for the Dome bringing emergency relief for a food shortage,' Tom read from his touchscreen. 'Any chance she stopped somewhere else – perhaps had malfunction.'

Peter shook his head.

'Despite what the rumours say there are no hidden entrances to these places. If she arrived at another colony they would have sent us a notification and we'd have contacted her. She never arrived.'

Tom shot Caleb a questioning look. Caleb nodded. It was safe to ask this man.

'Peter, what we're about to tell you is confidential,' Tom began.

The dock-master's brow furrowed.

'What's going on?'

'We believe Eleanor may have gone off planet,' Caleb finished.

Peter drew a breath and let it out in a whistle.

'Oh Mary. She'll lose her license...'

'Not of her own volition,' Caleb said quickly. Peter's furrowed brow deepened.

'You mean she was forced?'

'Yes. Now, it's very important that you give us an accurate answer to this next question Peter.'

Peter puffed out his chest.

'Fire away.'

'Do you know exactly who was on her ship with her when it left?'

'Aye,' he said. 'It was her and Jim. Jim's her co-pilot, been with her for years like. Not sure if there was another. I can check the freight papers if you like?'

'Please.'

They waited in silence as Peter scrolled through the records stored on his device. Caleb was sweating uncontrollably.

'That's strange,' Peter said.

'What?'

Caleb's lips felt parched. His heart beat irregularly in his chest as though it'd forgotten how.

'There *was* someone else.' He tapped the screen. 'Says here it was the prison warden of o-six: Hank Marshall.'

<>ACCESS LOGS</>
  <>PSYCHOLOGICAL   CLINIC   AUSTIN   POLICE   DEP.
TEXAS EARTH</>
  <>RECORD NO. 659</>
  <>CREATED 08:01:02 23/10/2058 EARTH TIME</>
  <>BEGIN RECORD</>

I DON'T THINK these sessions are necessary anymore, Doc.

What are we achieving here? You can't make my wife forgive me and you can't help me catch him so what the fuck are we doing here?

I don't have a condition you can diagnose. I'm not going to neatly tick all the boxes of paranoia. I'm a detective. That's what I am. That's who I am. If you don't mind I'm going back to my desk.

<>RECORDED SUSPENDED</>

DAY 59

23RD FEBRUARY 2068

Eleanor pulled herself weightlessly down the main deck. Behind her, Jim watched from the door to his cabin, one leg planted on the deck in a magnetic boot and the other drifting like a lame tail. Eleanor halted her flight by gripping the two handholds on each side of the corridor. The magnetic boots were far too noisy for what she wanted to do and so she put her pilot's training to good use. In the old days they'd never had mag-boots anyway.

She let go of one of the handholds and swung herself around, when she got close enough she reached out and used her fingertips on the cabin door to silently slow herself. She judged it well. Her ear hovered inches from the door. She listened.

At first she wasn't sure she could hear anything except the low throb of the electrical pulse moving through the craft. She closed her eyes and opened her ears, a meditative technique she'd learned to enhance awareness. Her thoughts relaxed so that all the sounds her brain normally blocked out as background came to the fore: A hiss as one of the adjusting thrusts kept their craft level. A creaking sound - the hull's metal responding to the warping cold.

Talking.

At first she couldn't make out any words. It began low and guttural like the opening to some religious chant in a distant epoch of earth's history. Eventually it changed and became higher, more melodic. It finished with something resembling a conversation but too quick to be natural. This was not half mumbled prayer words or a recitation memorised by rote, it was a fully fledged conversation with pitch modulation, change of tone, questioning, the occasional fragment that stood out from the rest as an unequivocal command often followed by cringing apologies.

It made Eleanor's skin crawl, because the man she now knew was Craig Smiley had entered the cabin alone. He had also locked the cabin from the inside, as he did every night. She could override the lock - it was her damn ship after all and no one could use it against her forever - but it would be noisy. He would hear it coming. For a start she'd have to go down into the maintenance shaft. She had to wait until he slept.

So far, she hadn't once found him sleeping, at any hour. Not for the first time she wondered whether he was playing a tape to trick her. Not for the first time she dismissed the idea. It was unmistakeably his voice and the conversations she overheard changed each time though they always began with a chant. Sometimes they were urgent, rapid, like two excited artists reaching the end of a long project and talking about the fruits it would bear. Other times they were soothing, like a hypnotherapy session.

She twisted and looked at Jim and shook her head. He sighed and hopped back into his room and locked the door. Eleanor made her way back along the corridor and pulled herself into her room. She strapped herself into the semi-upright bed and tried to forget what had happened over the last week.

When she'd come to after being knocked out she'd been strapped into the pilot's chair facing Jim. Jim was still unconscious and his knee had been treated with heal-aid cream and sutured with a needle and thread from the medical kit. She'd thought Jim had done it until she realised he was unconscious. It must have been Smiley.

A shadow had obscured her view of Jim.

'I may not be a pilot,' Craig said. 'But I know I only need one of you to man this junker.' He crouched down so his eyes were level with hers and she thought of how much like a feral creature he looked beneath the uniform. 'You get to decide which one of you I have to torture to make the other do it for me.'

'You don't have to torture anyone,' she said. 'I'll fly her for you.'

Smiley nodded and stood. He circled around behind Jim and placed a hand on his shoulder. Jim groaned as though a sudden pain had bloomed and reached even his unconscious mind. His eyelids flickered.

'If you double cross me,' Smiley said. 'I will hurt him. If you raise an alarm. I will hurt him. If you try to escape. I will do things to his body you cannot imagine –'

'I understand,' she said, unable to keep the desperation out of her voice.

With the measure of a planet spinning, Smiley shook his head. The eyes pushed into her own as though forcing them back into her head.

'No, you don't. You think I'm doing this because I'm evil, Captain Cole. But I assure you, I intend to heal earth. My aim is pure, you see. These officers of the law and prison wardens and guards stand in my way and so I have resorted to violence and deception but if they had allowed me to finish my work things would have been different. So different...'

Eleanor looked at her captor and the strange half-light shining in his eyes. It made her think of a dying world baked into a radioactive glow by an overpowering sun. There was a twist of sorrow in his voice as he spoke.

It was at that moment she realised he was utterly insane.

It was not a madness that'd warped a once healthy mind. On the contrary, his mind had grown from the madness like some ill-formed amphibian slinking out of the fertile pool of origin. When Eleanor's mother had developed dementia later in her life, it'd made her paranoid, afraid to go out. She lost her sense of person and place and forgot things Eleanor thought no one could ever forget. In the end, when she'd looked into her mother's eyes, she hadn't seen her mother but a dull, corrosive entity that'd eaten away everything inside her and then nestled in to animate the body. This was not what she saw in Smiley. What she saw now was a being *made* of madness.

She could not break his stare despite trying.

'What are you going to do?'

He smiled.

'Open the Black Gate.'

As Eleanor lay strapped into her bed, those words turned over and over in her head like some endless chant sung out of the deepest time echoing through to the present. Eventually the chant lulled her to sleep though she slept without resting. Her dreams were full of mirrors and shadows and doorways opening onto dark planes that held deeper darkness within them. At the end of the dream she thought she saw a bone-thin man with a strange crown walking across the darkness towards her.

And behind the man with the crown walked her mother.

The next morning Eleanor got up and attended to her daily wash routine and did an hour of mag-weight exercise and went into the pilot room.

'Good morning, Captain Cole.'

She twisted and stumbled back.

She hadn't noticed Smiley was already there because he sat in the shadow of the corner of the room as though part of it. He spoke with the air of a fellow guest at an expensive hotel greeting her at the breakfast table, as though it was nothing at all. She now understood something of what Jim had said. She *hated* Smiley. Not just for what she now knew he was: a murderer, a torturer, a criminal, but also because everything in her felt repulsed by him. It was like she was living some old moralistic tale – for wanting money she now had to suffer and for how long she did not know.

She sat down at the controls and turned her back to him. She looked out at the darkness and the stars and felt a little comfort in their light. At least she was home. At least she was where she belonged. She could see this through just as she'd seen everything else through. Whilst her hands were on the controls and her ship hummed beneath her, things were not entirely bad. She wondered whether that feeling of having something warm and strong and powerful under her control was why some women loved horses so much. Maybe *Penelope* was her horse. Faithful to the last. Not a bad name for one either. Only horses had never interested Eleanor. They couldn't fly, for a start.

'I trust you slept well?' he said, breaking in on her thoughts. For a moment she'd managed to forget the shadow.

'Fine.'

'Never take up a career in sales, Eleanor. You are a terrible liar.'

She tore her eyes away from the deep of space and looked at him. There was a glossy coating over his eyes like varnish. All seemed well and good on the surface. But Eleanor had learned how to look a little deeper. She wondered how she hadn't seen it when she first laid eyes on him. Maybe it'd been because she was drunk. Maybe it was the 2K30 helmet or the low lighting of the Rock Biter. Either way, there was something behind the gloss which was frightening like a tar-choked pool. No matter what way you looked at the eyes you could not un-see it: a deep well like an open mouth. True oblivion.

'What do you want from me?'

'My father worked in sales,' he said, ignoring the question. 'Worked his whole life selling products. Selling himself. Selling lies. Do you want to know what that taught me?'

She swallowed. A part of her did, because a part of her could not shirk the terrible fascination in every human being with things gone wrong.

'That nothing means anything?' she said. 'That we're all soulless? Some existential bullshit.'

Smiley sat forward in his seat so his head emerged into the dull light.

'Not at all,' he said. 'Quite the contrary. We *do* have souls. And this world,' he pointed out at the dark expanse outside the pilot window. 'Is a thin veil pulled over the bare skin of a living god. We can see the vague shape of the god. We can hear the words of the god. We can almost feel the god sometimes. But we can never fully see. We can never fully touch. And we can never truly hear. When the god moves our universe moves around it. All our actions are echoes of the real world which lies beyond the Black Gate. There is no substance only the physical symptom of purpose and intent. Do you understand?'

She looked into his eyes and shook her head.

'No.'

Smiley reclined back into his shadow.

'You will do.' He sighed. 'Before this journey is done. You will do.'

<>ACCESS LOGS</>
   <>MARS CONTAINMENT FACILITY 006</>
   <>RECORD NO. 101004</>
   <>CREATED 09:06:02 26/12/2060 EARTH TIME</>
   <>BEGIN RECORD</>

Do I believe it's wrong?

Well, Detective Marvin, that leads to a rather obvious answer. No. I don't believe it's wrong. I wouldn't have done it otherwise. You see, human beings as a species are an anomaly. Every other creature knows its purpose. You watch the humble bee moving from flower to flower. You watch it scoop up the pollen with its legs, diligent, attentive, absorbed in what it needs to do. It makes no mistakes. It fulfils its role absolutely. And at the end of its chores it produces something beautiful. Honey. Sweet and delicious.

You watch human beings however and see something very different. You watch them toiling in the fields, labouring in the factories amidst the machines that build places like this and you realise we have forgotten how to produce honey.

Tell me, what does a butcher produce now? A sack of cancerous meat shipped off to some nameless company and in turn consumed by ignorant tasteless masses. What does a factory worker produce? The component of a machine that one day will replace him. Art has become meaningless – the tool of the wealthy to promote their own political ideology or condemn their opponents'. The poor cannot afford to produce it, either with time or money, and when they do it is ugly because their lives are ugly. So you see: we do not produce honey anymore.

We live in a culture that has accepted and indeed enshrined the belief that invisible values counted by governments and computers determine what we are worth to each other and ourselves. We believe buying is equivalent to earning.

It's no different for those in the upper echelons of society: the managers, the deputies, the egomaniacal scientists who have become our golden rams. They write books, marry trophy wives, design new rockets to take curious millionaires to Mars in record time, but their mind is on other things. They have everything and yet they wake up hungrier than the poorest soul on earth. They want something from life but they just don't know how to look for it. From day to day they trudge through their monotonous minds and thoughts, enraged by who they are and not even knowing it. They turn to substances. Drink numbs self actualisation. Drugs solidify fantasies of identity.

But everyone sobers up some time and then they're left with the hole in their bellies they'll never fill. Ever wondered why so many so-called brilliant minds die young? They might not put a blade to their wrists but they kill themselves all the same.

You want to know why?

It's because they serve themselves and only themselves. We are a race of Narcissuses. This is how we are profoundly alien to our own world. The humble bee, buzzing from flower to flower, is serving something higher than itself. That is what gives the humble bee purpose. That is what gives the humble bee power.

Did you know that in the ancient culture of the Aztecs there was a fertility ritual that required the sacrifice of captured warriors? The captives were killed, flayed, and then their skin was worn by the priests for twenty days. All of this was done to bring prosperous harvests to the land.

Now no doubt you condemn such practice as the work of savages. I'll admit to a modern western mind filled up with delusions of logic and reason it might seem pointless, irrational, a waste of life. Isn't that the phrase the news-readers love? "A terrible waste". As if they are authorised to judge the value of a person's soul.

But let's say for a moment that the Aztec gods are real. Let's say their power is derived from sacrifice. Let's say that without these sacrifices their power wanes and the vital life of the land wanes with it. Crops will die. People will starve. When people go hungry they will fight with each other for food. The wars of the last twenty years are a prime example of it. China half tore itself apart once water started to look thin on the ground, didn't it?

So, without purpose, there is chaos. There is theft. Bloodshed. Civilisation falls apart. The angry and strong prevail. The weak and innocent die. Order is overturned, and quicker than you might think. All of this could have been avoided if the god had been appeased.

Make no mistake, Detective Marvin. I quite agree with you. The Aztec gods are not true gods. That is why we stopped believing in them. That is why they couldn't feel the spider even when it had already pushed its venom into their arteries.

But that is not to say there are no gods. "Once you eliminate the impossible, whatever remains, no matter how improbable, must be the truth."

I have eliminated the impossible, Detective Marvin. That is why I have purpose. That is why there must be sacrifices.

For the longest time I couldn't understand why people were afraid of me and my work. Now I do. I offer them purpose, meaning, truth, yet they spit in my face. They do so because they are afraid of becoming nothing, afraid of surrendering their selves to something higher. What they don't realise is they had nothing to surrender. They have defined themselves with extraneous toys, objects to fill the emptiness in their heads which serve no greater good than their own interest.

You've seen space, Detective Marvin. Consider it a rare gift. There was a time not long before we were born when no one could have imagined even getting to the moon. Now we've got facilities on Mars. It might just be prisons and mines for now but that won't keep the people happy for long.

The thing is, despite everything, we've missed the most important lesson space should have taught us. When you look out there into the blackness you see the great big abyss that is in ourselves. But it is not entirely empty. It is not godless. There is order in the stars. There is crystal clarity. Light shining. There has to be, don't you think?

I bet when you shipped out here in one of those GC Transports you looked back at the big blue mother-Earth in the rear window just like me and thought about our place in the universe. Hard not to, isn't it?

You saw the truth through that rad-resistant glass: we're nothing but fungus sprouting on some wet, warm rock surrounded by an infinite expanse of cosmic radiation, black holes, meteorites. Somehow we keep on spinning. And I say we only keep spinning because we were *put* on earth.

How'd it happen? Could have happened any number of ways, Detective. Those big meteorites they found up in Antarctica for a start. They had traces of life. Blasted to Earth from somewhere else in the universe by some unknown force.

Anyway, I'm getting away from the real point and you look tired Detective. I'd ask you why but I'm sure you wouldn't say.

Did you know the three-hundred-and-sixty-first day of the year is a special day in the Aztec calendar? It marks the beginning of the Nemontemi: a five day period preceding the New Year where only the worst things can happen, where the outcome of every action is a disaster. So you might not be entirely to blame for recent misfortune. I hope that comforts you.

You see, in the time of the Aztecs, during this period, people locked up their daughters and wives, rationed what food they had left from the winter, and hid from the world until it turned New Year. Quite different from our tradition, isn't it? But still, I should be grateful to be locked away on a barren rock at this time in the year.

Is it over already? And we'd only just gotten started. I enjoyed our chat and I have so much more to tell you about my work.

<>RECORD TERMINATES</>

Day 122

'I'm sure,' Caleb said, wishing that he wasn't.

Chief Justin Walker swore and his face turned blotchy on the videoscreen.

'This is bad Caleb. The lockdown came straight from Command. This could close the colonies if we don't pitch it right.'

'You know what the mines are like Justin. They think it's the wild-west out here.'

Justin sighed.

'Ok. I'll tell Command it was a professionally worked forgery the dock controllers couldn't have seen through and that the suspect had hostages. That ought to give them pause. I'll also notify Defence and see if they can get a track on that junker number. Provided he's not removed the inbuilt locator we should be able to pick him up soon as he lands.'

Caleb nodded. The monitor's camera only showed him from the shoulders up. If he'd been sat further away Justin would have been able to see his hand shaking like an addict's.

'I think we also need to make contact with the junker. If the dock-master's records are anything to go by Smiley left the Iron Caves eighty-one days ago. A lot could have happened in that time.'

Justin paused a moment and looked at Caleb as though truly looking at him for the first time in the conversation. When he did that, Caleb always had the sensation that Justin was measuring the weight of his heart and integrity like some modern Anubis. He even looked a little jackal-like.

Beneath the visibility of the screen, the detective's hand trembled violently. He kept his eyes even.

'Good idea,' the Chief said. 'I'll set up a wire team to record the call.'

Caleb breathed a sigh of relief inside his head.

'I'll hail the junker to discuss terms.'

Justin nodded.

The screen flashed and went dark. Caleb sat back in his chair and breathed as though he'd been submerged for the duration of the call. The inside of the empty GC was quiet as a holy place and so he closed his eyes and enjoyed the silence for a moment.

He knew calling the junker was the right thing to do. If Smiley had already killed one of the hostages or even both then they needed to know. Caleb suspected he wouldn't have. Resourceful though he was, he was a soldier and not a pilot and he doubted he could fly the junker without Eleanor or Jim, her co-pilot. Still, they needed to be sure.

Caleb was also concerned about how badly he *wanted* to call the junker. It was strange but in listening to the interviews over and over he had an urge to hear Smiley's voice again. He remembered those interviews like the most haunting of his dreams, the way Smiley had so causally told him why he'd done what he'd done, the way he'd described violence like it was religion.

Up until now he and Tom had been chasing after a fox that'd already dug under the fence. When he'd worked the case seven years ago Caleb had almost been driven insane by it, and yet, at no other point in his life had he felt he had such purpose. It was a feeling no one or thing had ever been able to give him again, not even Martha. And he knew it was linked to Smiley in more ways than just as a challenging case. The purpose *came* from Smiley, as though Caleb had become part of his dark web.

'Get out of my head,' he said, to nothing. He looked at his hands and saw they were still shaking. He knew the councillor had done his best but the damage was too deep to be articulated and he doubted it could ever be healed.

He shook himself and stood and left the GC to find Tom.

He found him hunched over a tall glass of whiskey in the Rock Biter. Caleb waved his hand to clear the purple vapour out of the air and pulled out a cigarette and lit it and sat down opposite Tom. He took a drag. Damn, it was the first cigarette he'd had in a long time and it felt good. His hands stopped shaking after his second drag.

Tom looked a mess. He was pale in a way that suggested he was fading away from solidity. His eyes were hollow and rimmed with shadow. Caleb couldn't help but think he was starting to look a lot like himself.

'What's up?'

Tom swigged.

'I fucked up.'

'We all fuck up.'

'Not you.' Tom brought the glass to his lips and paused to stare down into the amber liquid, as though he'd seen something there. Then he gulped the remainder down. Despite how much Caleb was reminded of the bawling Hank Marshall he was quite impressed at just how much whiskey Tom could stomach in a single swallow. 'You're the perfect fucking detective.'

'No. If I was the perfect detective I'd have a drinking problem as well as narcotic one.' He held up his cigarette as though toasting and took another drag.

Tom gave a high pitched laugh.

'Yeah, maybe I should divorce Melinda, or get her to divorce me, then I'd be real detective material.'

'Or just a loser.'

Tom gave him a sharp look and Caleb sensed he was not as drunk as he seemed. He also became aware Tom was a big guy and could probably throw a punch like a donkey's back-kick.

He leant forward over the table.

'Listen Tom, you made a call and I made a call and we both had our reasons. You may not have been right about Smiley but let me tell you something: you were right about me.'

Tom put his elbows on the table and met Caleb eye to eye.

'What do you mean?'

'I'm...' Caleb gritted his teeth and whistled through them. 'I'm...I'm in deep. Ever since Martha, you know...'

Tom nodded and reached for his glass, only to realise it was empty. He looked nervous, as though half expecting Caleb to explode and start shooting up the bar.

Caleb blinked.

'Ever since Martha I've been thinking about this case over and over and re-reading those damn poems he wrote and listening to the interviews and then...one day...'

'He escaped,' Tom finished.

Caleb paused and looked into the purple smog and in it he saw more than the shadows of people but the shadows that inhabited dreamscapes. He closed his eyes.

'I feel like *I* set him free.'

A hand clamped down on his arm and he half jumped out of his skin. Tom looked strong and firm and though he was still pale his eyes shone a little brighter.

'That's crazy talk, Cal. Maybe it was just a hunch. I ain't one for believing in a god, but I think sometimes people feel things outside themselves. After all, we were all part of one atom once.'

Caleb nodded.

'I hope so.'

'You can't live with the guilt of him escaping so don't put it on yourself. Anyway, Hank Marshall is gonna be a lot higher on the list of those responsible than you are. Like, getting ass-raped in hell higher.'

Caleb burst out laughing.

'I don't think anyone deserves to get ass-raped in hell.'

Tom shrugged.

'Smiley?'

Caleb frowned and took a final drag on his cigarette and stubbed it out.

'No,' he stood up. 'If anything the devil's paying him to do the raping. You coming back to the GC?'

'You're gunna hail the junker, aren't you?'

'Hell yeah.'

It took them twenty minutes to locate junker-0329's frequency and lock onto it. ELD (Extreme Long Distance) communications like this had been made possible by the discovery in the 20s of a mechanism of boosting signal strength over time by having the signals bounce off each other to get further with each broadcast. Caleb understood little about the actual science behind it but a techy in Austin had once told him it was almost like throwing grappling hooks onto a boat. At first, you only had one grapple attached and the connection was weak, but then you threw a second and a third and the connection grew. More grapples could then be applied by moving along the ones previously thrown and then attaching them until it was more like a small bridge.

Tom sat out of camera shot but had his monitor open and was analysing the call – both the strength of the broadcast and, when it began, vocal fluctuations which would let them know if Smiley was lying. Justin dropped them an instant message when the wire team put the tap in place on their line. Caleb breathed and went into himself. On his second deep breath he choked and coughed. Damn cigarette, he thought.

'Ready when you are,' Tom said.

'Go.'

They began hailing. There were four or five unanswered hails before the line was picked up and the connection held.

'This is Captain Cole of the *Penelope*.' It was a female voice – Caleb knew instantly this was the real Eleanor Cole although he looked at Tom who gave him an a-ok sign to confirm the voice match. Surprisingly she sounded calm but he wondered whether that was strength of character more than anything else.

'Hello Captain Cole,' Caleb said, keeping his voice smooth. 'My name is Detective Caleb Rogers of the Austin Police Department, acting under the authorisation of Interplanetary Command.'

'Hello Detective Rogers,' she said. 'How can I help you?'

'Slight fluctuation,' Tom whispered.

'We have come to believe there might be a stowaway aboard your vessel –'

'Detective –'

The line cut off. Caleb repeated the words 'Captain Cole' but there was no answer. Just as he was about to swipe his hand across the screen and end the call he heard breathing that cracked the receiver.

He exchanged a glance with Tom.

He *knew* that breathing in the same way he'd recognise the voice of a parent or a long time teacher; it reached inside him and plucked at a buried web of memory causing ripples and tremors to pass along each strand and through his whole body. It disturbed and rattled his thoughts. Even though he thought he had prepared he was not prepared. His palm became slick with sweat and the shaking returned.

'Detective Rogers, and I'm assuming Detective Marvin as well? It's been a long time.'

The voice made Caleb think of the long-dead Lazarus only just brought into life again, the voice of something that should be dead.

'I must say,' the voice continued. 'I am impressed. I thought for a while I would reach Earth and no one would be any wiser. It would've made things easier, but then, things easily done are not worth doing.'

'It's over,' Caleb said, with more confidence than he had. 'Earth Defence has surface to air missiles locked onto your craft and the second you enter atmosphere you will be shot down. You might as well turn yourself in.'

The voice laughed. It sounded like white-noise on an old 20th century television screen.

'On the contrary, you have just heard Captain Cole's voice: I doubt you are about to blow this aircraft out of the sky. Jim McLeod is also still alive. I do not kill for pleasure or needlessly. You of all people should know that. How many hours did we spend running over and over it in that interview room on Mars, eh Detective Rogers? You couldn't get enough. I almost thought I'd found a disciple!'

Caleb felt his shaking hands become fists. He unclenched them and let out a slow breath.

'Detective Marvin seemed less interested in the order of the cosmos,' the voice went on. 'I suppose he was keen to get back to fucking the prison attendant. I imagine she looks a lot like his wife. They fired her because of that little fling, by the way. But I suppose you don't give a shit, do you detective? Because you're still employed.'

Caleb forced himself not to look at Tom.

'For me to become your disciple, you'd have to have a religion. You don't. What you have is undiagnosed schizophrenia.'

The silence that followed told Caleb his jab had found its mark. He and Tom listened to the breathing thicken and drop.

'You don't know anything, detective.'

'Massive spike,' Tom said, shakily. 'Keep hitting him.'

'On the contrary,' Caleb continued. 'We know everything. We know you are on board junker-0329: *Penelope*. We know you are just over 30 days from Earth. We also know that you have a single heavy calibre weapon with limited ammo capacity and that you have two hostages. Considering you need your hostages to pilot the ship I'd say all of this puts you in a very bad position. But then again, brains are never the strong point of the criminally insane. Didn't you first think up your bullshit gods in an insane asylum?'

A scream tore the line and left crackling fizzles of static behind it. Caleb thought the call was over but to his surprise the scream trailed out and was replaced by asthmatic breathing – Caleb could hear the rattling effort of control with each sucking breath.

'You are forgetting something: I may need my hostages to pilot the ship, but I never threatened to kill them. There is a lot I can do to them that won't stop them being able to land this craft.'

'If you torture them now you're only doing it for pleasure,' Caleb said quickly. 'That makes you a hypocrite.'

A pause.

'I really did think that you would understand what it means to put faith in something higher. You *think* you have faith in your god but you don't. When your wife died you received the call to strike out against the wrongs of the world but did *nothing*. You think being a detective means you are "right", but you're even more lost than the petty criminal. I'm following a call, detective Rogers. You must follow yours.'

The screen flashed to show the connection had been severed. Caleb felt weariness descend on him as though he'd just competed in a marathon. His bones ached in a way that made him think of endless time passing: like all the years falling on Dorian Gray at once. He looked over at Tom.

'They'll be playing that one in the training seminars,' Tom said.

'I hope not,' he said. 'I almost flunked it.'

'No, you did good,' Tom said and offered one of his rare, boyish smiles.

'Thanks.'

Caleb sat down and lay his head back in his seat and closed his eyes for a moment. He imagined the storm that he'd cooked up in Smiley and what that meant. Sure, he was probably going to make a mistake and that'd been the whole aim, but storms also created collateral damage.

And no one could say when they were going to stop.

<>ACCESS LOGS</>
   <>MARS CONTAINMENT FACILITY 006</>
   <>RECORD NO. 102009 – SUBSEQUENTLY DELETED</>
   <>CREATED 00:03:00 25/01/2061 EARTH TIME </>
   <>BEGIN RECORD</>

MELINDA.

I have something to tell you.

I don't know how to say it and I don't want to hurt you.

I've made a mistake. A big mistake. I...

Fuck. I don't even know where to begin. I thought I was a good husband. Hell, I thought I was a good man. But I'm not. I'm just another loser. I fucked up.

Shit, how can I tell you?

I can't even tell myself.

<>RECORD TERMINATES</>

Day 156

23RD May 2068

Smiley balled his hands into fists and smashed them one after another into the metal wall of the cabin and choked on his own screams. With every punch he imagined breaking the stupid detective's face, imagined the nose cracking apart and washing the upper lip with blood, imagined the lip splitting like torn bread and revealing broken teeth and bleeding gums. He imagined then putting the heavy calibre to his temple and pulling the trigger and washing the ground with his brains.

No, that was too quick.

He imagined breaking his fingers and toes one by one and then smashing his head on concrete until it broke open like a shattered egg and spilled brains.

It was weeks on and he still couldn't get his mocking words out of his head.

For me to become your disciple, you'd have to have a religion.

Smiley howled and tore a clump of his hair clean out of his head and the burn across his scalp only fuelled the rage. His knuckles were white and bleeding but he pounded the wall harder.

The worst thing was he was snared. How could he now go and hurt his hostages knowing he would be going against everything he'd said he stood for in those long, drawn out interviews?

He slumped against the wall, his head resting against the cool metal. His hands trembled with the pain but he did not allow himself the weakness of responding to that pain.

He tried to think back to who Caleb Rogers was. He remembered he was a widower. He remembered the smell of cigarette smoke and silence. That was the thing. With Marvin it'd been endless questions on questions as if he thought by asking questions he was achieving something. Caleb Rogers had *listened*...

This wasn't enough. He had to *understand* him. He had to think like the man he wanted to destroy to know where he would hide, where he would run, what tactics he would use. Once he'd been pretty sure he knew the detectives like a favourite story but years had gone by and he'd forgotten. Yet this was a new game not an old one played again. A game – like chess. White and black pieces in an eternal conflict: the modern lie of light and dark being against one another when in fact light first bloomed in the darkness. Tom Marvin's flaxen hair – almost white - and Caleb Rogers - black haired. Black eyed. A crow. The Funeral Man. Death. He was a dead man walking. That was how Craig would beat him. He would show him he was a dead man walking and would gain nothing by stopping him. But he could live again. Yes. Born again as the Christians called it.

Caleb wasn't his only concern however. He also had to consider the co-pilot.

The heal-aid had done its work and he was almost walking normally now. A few more days and he'd practically be bounding. Then Smiley would have a problem. Even though he had locked away the sword-cane in his own cabin he suspected Jim had other tricks up his leave. Smiley hated to admit it, but he was unnerved by him. Maybe because he'd suspected him from the start or maybe because that night in the Rock Biter he'd talked the same way Smiley did: about ideas. He'd have to kill Jim soon and he wouldn't be breaking his word. He was doing it to protect himself. To protect the mission.

Maybe he should do it now. Get it over with.

The craft gave a lurch and Smiley only just remained standing. The ship gave another gentler heave. He knew it wasn't a twist of the steering controls. It was a buffet.

Gravity.

Earth.

He grabbed the rifle and keyed in the code to his cabin door, unlocking it. He sealed the door shut behind him and moved as quickly as he could up the deck to the pilot room. He barged in and saw what he'd waited seven years to see: a blue, luminous sphere glowing like the radiant face of Krishna. He could not suppress the gasp that came to his lips. He stood transfixed, face lit as though by a ritual flame, speechless and humbled. *So close!* If he raised his rifle and fired through the viewing port his bullets would tear country-wide holes in the floating ball before him. How could it be this close after being nothing more than an over-bright star glimpsed through the teeth of blast doors?

But even in that awe-struck moment Smiley didn't entirely let his guard down. He saw a flickering movement out of the corner of his eye and twisted, lithe as a cat.

This twist saved him from being knocked out cold by Jim who had just swung a hammer with all his might at the back of his skull. Instead, he clipped Smiley's shoulder and neck and sent him reeling.

Eleanor was up from the console in a flash and running towards him. Smiley raised the gun but she slapped it aside. He realised the gun was heavier than he remembered and cursed as it slipped out of his fingers.

Eleanor did not stop there. She drove a sharp stomping kick into the inside of his leg. He growled and was knocked down to one knee feeling as though a tendon would snap at any moment. He saw the hammer descend again and quick as a child snatching at a butterfly he caught it at the handle. It felt like a bamboo shoot had been stabbed all the way up his arm from the webbed skin between thumb and index to his elbow but he did not let go. He forced himself to stand and twisted the hammer out of Jim's grip and swung it wildly, forcing Eleanor and the co-pilot to jump back.

Then it was his turn.

Driven delirious by pain and rage he came on frothing at the mouth, only dimly aware that if he killed them now he would not be able to land the craft. As he swung the hammer at Jim he caught another glimpse of the blue shining face of Krishna looking at them through the pilot's window: beneficent and yet oblivious.

Jim raised both his arms to shield his head and Smiley smashed the hammer into his forearm. The co-pilot screamed and fell back clutching his arm. Bone burst out from the skin, ragged at the end like a snapped tree-branch. Smiley wheeled on Eleanor and swung. She was more agile and ducked and evaded his wild swings.

'Come here you fucking bitch!'

Finally he swung a heavy downward blow which she side stepped and his hammer smashed into a screen on the control panel sending splintering glass cascading across the floor. He felt a stab of pain in the back of his leg, then another and he tried to turn but instead tumbled to his knees. She was doing something to his muscles. Incapacitating him. Hitting him at pressure points. The bitch was fucking trained.

He flailed with his hammer and she backed away.

She was trembling and sweat-flecked but he saw a steel in her eyes like the steel of the ship's infrastructure and for a moment the rage ebbed with a glimmer of admiration. Craig Smiley valued only faith over courage.

He clambered to his feet. Jim sobbed, clutching his broken arm. Eleanor backed away keeping her eyes trained on him. He stole a quick glance behind and saw the great blue-face expanding behind them. They were being drawn down into atmosphere. He thought of the mass of the sea and realised the world could almost be the colourful centre of a whirlpool amidst the blackness.

'Nice try,' he said. 'But no more games.'

Eleanor backed away further from him; she sank into a boxing stance. Smiley couldn't stop his lips curling back to reveal teeth. If this is the way you want it, he thought. I may only need one.

'Yes...no more games...'

Smiley turned and saw Jim was sitting upright with the heavy calibre SA101 resting in the crook of his elbow. His good hand was on the trigger. He looked like a heroin addict: white faced, dripping with sweat, trembling as though his every effort was just to keep himself from shooting up his next fix. But the gun was evenly trained on him. His eyes were hard as ice.

'If you shoot me,' Smiley said, slowly. 'You will also shoot through me and shatter the windscreen. Then we all die. Even your precious Eleanor...'

Jim blinked.

'It's worth us both dying,' Eleanor said.

Smiley looked from one to the other. He burst out laughing. Jim growled and tightened his finger on the trigger but Smiley knew he wouldn't pull it.

'Look at you: like a fucked up Romeo and Juliet who aren't even fucking.' He grinned. 'Go on then, Jim. Kill the monster with a twitch of your finger.' He held out his arms wide. 'Send me back to the stars.'

'Do it Jim,' Eleanor said, soft as a mother. 'Do it.'

Jim shook more violently. He gritted his teeth.

There was no shot.

'What are you –'

But before Eleanor could finish her sentence Smiley threw his hammer hard as he could and caught her on the temple sending her slumping to the ground like a droid whose power had been disconnected. Jim roared. Smiley kicked the gun out of his hand and then stamped on his broken arm.

The scream that tore from Jim's throat made Smiley hard. That was what he wanted to hear from the so-called fucking hero.

But Jim wasn't done. He threw himself backwards and scissored his legs, trapping Smiley's. They struggled for a moment, Smiley trying to disentangle himself, but Jim was burly and grounded. The ship gave a gigantic lurch upwards and he heard a snapping noise as though they'd just punched through a thin sheet of ice that circled the world.

Unbalanced, he hit the deck, hard, and slid down towards the controls. The ship was slowly tipping forward, heading into a nose dive. Scrambling to gain footing he grabbed the lip of the control panel and pushed himself up in time to see Jim making for the gun. The ship's tilt grew more violent. He ran up the forty-five degree slope and rugby tackled Jim to the ground and they both went flying. Both tried to rise, but neither could get their feet off the ground.

Jim realised it first. He started unbuckling his magnetic boots. Smiley reached for his own, fumbling with the straps. He became savage, tearing like a cat trying to claw its way out of a cardboard box, but Jim was over him before he got the second one off and started clubbing him with the metal edge of his boot. Needle pain dug into Smiley's scalp and he felt blood run down his face like bitter honey. He saw the edge of Jim's boot redden as though a brush dipped in a paint-pot. He slapped aside Jim's relentless hand on the fourth or fifth hit - he'd lost count how many times he'd been struck. He grabbed Jim's throat and stared into the blue eyes: eyes like the round widening Earth in the window.

For a second those eyes perturbed him, like a warning sign. He felt danger. He felt Jim's weapon-hand slipping away from his grasp. Tunnel-vision closed him to all else but those eyes that were also the world. He thought of his apocalypse, of his world crumbling and ending.

'People like you make hell real,' Jim spat.

Craig Smiley choked and felt the hand holding Jim's throat slip and then Jim's forehead smashed into the bleeding wound on his head and he screamed for the pain. Jim cracked his head against him again and this time it caught the centre of his head. Jim was bleeding from the head too now but he looked triumphant, like an Aztec priest about to wrench out the heart of his offering. The pain blossomed in the centre of Smiley's forehead, right where his third eye was, right where the finger of darkness had first touched. He blinked. He could feel the ship tipping.

Jim brought his head down again but Smiley twisted and snapped his elbow in Jim's face and blood exploded from his nose and he squealed.

'There is no hell,' he snarled, wrapping his arm around Jim's neck. 'Only godlessness.' He twisted and heard a crack loud as a rodeo whip. Jim's body jerked like a beheaded fish. At last, it went limp. Smiley looked at the corpse then spat on it and threw it aside. Jim's eyes stared up blankly at the ceiling and the azure sharpness that'd so frightened Smiley was gone.

He lay without motion feeling like a corpse himself. He could feel the ship drifting into freefall. He tried to look around him for a way out but he couldn't see anything except his father's face hovering over him saying words over and over again.

You sick little boy. You sick little boy. You sick little boy.

That was what his father had said to him the first time he'd caught him looking at girls. *Sick little boy.* That was all anyone had ever thought of him. *Undiagnosed schizophrenic. Madman. Madman. Sick little boy.* But he wasn't sick. He could just see what no one else could: the death in everyone's hearts. And he could see the way to end that death. Yes. Truth.

He pulled off his remaining mag-boot and stood. The immense globe was no longer visible. Instead, a massive plate of land beneath like a yellow shard of glass. A light bleeped on a satellite map of Earth on the control panel. One look told him it was the point marked by his coordinates. He looked at the empty pilot's wheel. He had no idea how to fly the junker but he now had no choice.

He clambered up and sat in the pilot's seat and put his hand to the pilot's wheel and began to steer it back on course. It was more of a strain than he could have ever thought. The ship started to rattle as he pulled out of the freefalling nose dive and the rattling went through his body, into the backs of his teeth, into the roots of every molar.

Hours he turned his hand to the wheel. Warning lights beeped on and off and the ship juddered as though trying to shake itself apart. He thought sometimes it was as though the junker was rebelling against his control. Finally he saw a line of dark forestry he knew marked a border between Texas and Louisiana, just north-east of Houston. He checked the coordinates again, doubting himself, and looked out of the window. The coordinates he'd found scratched on the cave in Mars could have led him anywhere in the world and yet they had led him back to the beginning, *his* beginning. A sensation like submerging in a glorious summer sea overcame him and he wept for joy. He was *meant* to do this – from his very *childhood* he had been chosen to open the gate. It was here, waiting for him. He had completed so much of the work before. He only had one more offering to make.

He took the junker lower.

Beneath him he saw lines and lines of squad cars speeding along almost every visible road and a helicopter moving towards him like a warrior-bee defending its hive.

A monitor on his left flashed to show an incoming call. He swiped his hand across it.

'Is this Captain Cole?'

'I have Captain Cole at gun point! You will not move to intercept me!'

There was a pause.

'Craig Smiley, you have escaped custody and violated the terms of your sentence. Comply and you will be returned to the facility on Mars without accruing further penalty.'

Smiley roared with laughter.

'It's already a life sentence,' he said. 'And there is no life in submission!' He swept his hand across the monitor to end the call.

The forest swelled and swelled as though a black cancerous growth sweeping across the sickening skin of the world. The squad cars followed his course as best they could. He wished this ship had guns so he could shred them like he used to shred troublesome ants with his BB gun as a kid. He thought of the way he'd used to light matches and drop them into the seething masses of black insects and watch them scatter.

An idea came to him.

The dark line of pines swelled and swelled. He couldn't land this ship and to do so would be a mistake. He left the controls and grabbed the heavy calibre machine gun. Then he picked up Eleanor and slung her over his shoulder and carried her down the deck and into his cabin. He strapped her into the zero-g bed and then returned to the pilot room. The front end of the junker was visible through the window and shone white-hot. Streaks of orange light coursed over it as though they flew inside a phoenix's tail. He grabbed Jim's mag-boots and hurried back to the cabin. He strapped the boots back on his feet and then put the other two on his hands clamped himself against the wall – limbs pulled into four points like Da Vinci's esoteric sketch. He breathed deep into his lungs and closed his eyes.

Impact.

DAY 238

C aleb sat amidst the smell of dust in a lightless room and looked down the barrel of his gun. He'd been sitting up all night in his suit looking into the gun and thinking.

In no way was he contemplating suicide. On the contrary, he was imagining what Craig Smiley would feel staring down the barrel of the gun right before Caleb pulled the trigger and blew his brains out over the pavement. Maybe that was too quick for someone like him, but Caleb wasn't into taking chances. Quick. Clean. No distractions or toying.

He couldn't understand how they'd lost him. Justin had allowed him to video-interview the police officers involved. All of them had said practically the same thing. The junker crash-landed. A gunfight ensued. Smiley had escaped into the woods in the wild stretch somewhere between Kirbyvill and Vidor on the border of Louisiana. Time and time again Caleb asked Justin and the other detectives on the ground about sniffer dogs, patrolmen, the forest rangers. There were six national parks within 300 kilometres and yet not a single one of their rangers had either disappeared or found anyone matching Smiley's description or

Eleanor's. He knew the woods around Louisiana were big but surely you couldn't lose a wanted felon in them? – otherwise criminals would be vanishing all the time.

Of course, all of the above was excluding one terrifying factor which frequently returned to stare Caleb full in the face like a demented reflection. It was the possibility that Craig Smiley was not insane and that a supernatural agency aided him. Fight it hard as he could, Smiley had slipped the net and avoided death so many times Caleb was almost unable to stop himself thinking there was something to it even if it was in Smiley's belief alone.

There he went again, admiring him.

He turned the gun around and slid it into the inside holster of his jacket. He felt more secure being able to wear it again. He also felt more secure knowing if he had Smiley at gun point like he had seven years ago he wouldn't cuff him this time. He'd kill him. He'd put a bullet in his brain and send him splattering to the floor. Fuck the consequences.

A razorblade of light fell in through the shuttered window of his apartment. The world was waking up but Caleb still felt like he was in an unsolvable dream. Justin had told him not to come in today, to let himself recover from the stresses of so much interplanetary travel.

He might as well have told him to stop breathing.

Caleb stood and went to the door rolling a cigarette as he went. Austin Police Department was only a ten minute walk from where he lived. After Martha had died he'd sold the old house and moved as close as he could. He had a new bride now. She was blind and she held a sword.

When he arrived at the station he thought there must have been a recent terrorist attack because the place was in tumult. Then he slowly gathered from fragments of conversations that this was all about Smiley. It'd taken Smiley shooting four cops for anyone to realise this was serious. Even Command was upping its game. A group of men in suits and with black folders stood by Justin's office. Caleb was sure they were outsourced detectives from San Antonio or Dallas brought on to help.

Around the figures of authority a swarm of blue-shirted officers ran around throwing paperwork left, right and centre. Caleb wondered how anyone could think nowadays. Justin charged towards him.

'I know what you're gonna say,' Caleb said, putting up a hand.

'And I'm still gunna say it anyway: what the fuck are you doing here?'

'Working,' he growled.

'Sleep-walking more like it,' Justin scoffed. 'Look at yourself. You even touched a razor since you heard the news? Come on: you're exhausted, you're angry, I think maybe you need to talk...'

'I'm *never* talking to the fucking psychiatrist again, do you hear me?'

Several officers turned. Most of them dropped into silence. The men who looked like outsourced detectives turned curious and imperious gazes on the two of them. Caleb didn't know where the strength for such an outburst had come from but he felt like a stud fucking two girls at once: all the blood was rushing through his body at a million miles an hour and he wouldn't stop for any money.

'I'm not crazy. I'm not delusional. I just want to put Smiley behind bars. Then I'll take as much holiday as you like, maybe even fuck off to England twice a year like in the old days. Hell, I'll even host a few drinks at my place time to time. I'm not going crazy Justin: I just *need* to do this.'

To Caleb's surprise, Justin nodded.

'You better start taking your holiday because it gives me a fucking hell of a headache when they audit employee health. Meet in my office in ten. If I think for a second you're drowsy I'm sending you home.'

Caleb nodded.

'Understood.'

He sat in the corner of Justin's office and the other detectives who'd come from elsewhere in Texas sat in the same chairs he and Tom Marvin had sat four months ago and received the news Smiley was free. Caleb wondered whether they smelled the same thing he smelled: the sweat of fear. It made Caleb think the society they lived in was run on fear: fears of being fired, fears of losing social face, fears of punishment and fears of being unable to take the law into your own hands. It was how Smiley triumphed – he used people's fear like a gorgon's stare to make them helpless. Beneath everyone's stupid concerns over bills and status were deeper foundational fears, fears of monsters. The true monsters did not go 'bump' in the night. You never heard them coming until you woke up with their hand over your mouth and their eyes boring into yours. You did not see them crawl out of the cupboard. They were already sitting on your bed with a knife between your legs hushing you to sleep as though they are about to sing you a lullaby, one you will never forget.

'Caleb headed up the investigations on Mars,' Justin was saying. He didn't know how long Justin had been talking but thankfully it seemed no one had asked him a question yet. 'He first alerted us to the fact the prisoner found a way to escape mars.'

One of the detectives was nodding and writing something down on a clipboard then looked up and gave Justin a narrow-eyed glare a match for his own.

'You understand Chief Walker this was a serious security breach. I'm almost disbelieving it was possible without the knowing involvement of the miners.'

The way he said the word *miners* made Caleb's skin crawl. He wasn't into class wars but there was a certain type of sneer that got his hackles up. Maybe he'd inherited it from his father.

Then something clicked: these weren't detectives helping on the case, they were lackeys from Command conducting a review. For a second Caleb wasn't sure whether to swear or burst out laughing. They were in the middle of the most important investigation in seven years and bureaucracy still found a way to worm its way in.

'Take it up with the Iron Caves,' Justin said, with a grimace that might have been an attempt at a winning smile.

'We will do,' the auditor said, with a sickly one to match.

The other auditor had a more relaxed posture and a sagging belly that flopped over his belt as though it'd given up trying to hold itself in place. His eyes however were just as sharp and glinting as his partner's: like flint.

'We're not trying to throw around any accusations: we're just trying to get a summary of the situation as it stands. The prisoner has not been apprehended. He is at large. We have had several opportunities to catch him. Think of it as a gauntlet. The aim of a gauntlet is to stop someone getting through by creating as many stages of resistance as possible...' He made shapes with his hands to indicate a series of barriers, but Caleb kept watching his eyes, which roamed elsewhere in the room. It was disconcerting, like watching a puppet controlled by two people who were doing different parts of a show. 'He escaped the prison and at that point should have been caught by Carla Bolton's search teams but was not found. According to your report Detective Rogers, he then sneaked aboard a freight ship, at which point he should have been identified and caught. He then landed at the Iron Caves at which point again he should have been identified and caught.' Caleb watched as a vein started to stick out in the auditor's neck. This one was not as relaxed as he seemed, he was what Caleb's psychotherapist would have called an 'implosive', someone who sucked up all the rage. 'He then spent over a month hiding out in the mines, at which point he *should have been apprehended*. He then...'

'We get the picture,' Justin snapped.

'And now having been at the location where the commandeered junker landed, your force was unable to bring him into custody. We are now back where we started. You lost him 82 days ago. He could be in another state by now.'

'Border patrol...'

'May have been alerted,' the auditor continued, bulldozering over him. 'But the ultimate responsibility of catching him lies with *you.*'

Caleb wasn't sure, but for half a second he was sure the auditor glanced at him when he said it. Then he realised that would be exactly what he wanted him to see.

'At no point was Detective Rogers or Marvin there at the same time the prisoner was. If they had been they would have identified him and taken him in. They've been chasing him months behind and gotten further than anyone else. We wouldn't even be here if it wasn't for them...'

'And where are we, Chief Walker?' The first auditor said, in a quiet voice.

Justin's mouth opened but no sound came out. He looked like he was about to explode.

'Sitting in an office talking bullshit,' Caleb said, standing. The auditors both turned slowly to look at him with looks of disgust on their faces that gave Caleb a buzz of triumph, like a cold beer after a day of training. 'I think you were right Chief I'm tired from all the travelling and need to lie down.'

He left without waiting.

He did not go to lie down.

First he went down to impounded evidence. He knew some items had been recovered from the wreckage of the *Penelope* and wanted to make a start there. After all, Justin had been right, up till now they'd been months behind and on the wrong planet. They were still behind but not quite so far and at least there was little chance of Smiley getting back to Mars now. Caleb also doubted he had gone across state, though he wasn't yet one hundred percent able to articulate why. It would come though, with time. He just needed to see the right puzzle pieces.

Kyle McGinnis sat like an ancient gargoyle at the end of the room, behind him standing the doors to the evidence locker and records department. A cup of coffee - black like some witch's poison - fumed on the table and a long golden chain dangled from his belt, at the end of which was the keycard. At first glance someone might think that Kyle was something like Hank Marshall. They were similar heights, similar builds and had the same round face graven with workmen's lines of worry. The difference was that Kyle had been custodian of the evidence and records departments for over twenty five years and in that time not a single piece of data or hard evidence had gone missing. Everything was documented and everything was by the book. Kyle didn't care so much for a digital revolution and filed everything hard copy so when they'd had a server crash in 2041 he'd been able to pick up the pieces faster than anyone else in the building.

'Rogers,' he said. 'Haven't seen you around lately. At least not in the flesh. You've been plenty on the news.'

He grinned and showed teeth like chiselled stalagmites. Kyle had lost most of his real ones in '38 when a drug addict tried to break into the evidence to get at some confiscated coke. Since then he'd had adamantine nashers installed.

Caleb crossed the room and shook his hand.

'How're you doin Gatekeeper?'

'As well as someone can be shaking hands with the Funeral Man,' he replied. 'You look like Death come to collect my soul.'

'Just checking out some evidence today Kyle. Souls are Fridays.'

'And where's mine going?'

'Depends on whether you show me what I need to see.'

'You drive a hard bargain Funeral Man. It's not sweet enough for me yet.'

'It wasn't a bargain it was a threat,' Caleb said, with a wink.

Kyle grunted.

'Probably why it didn't work then.'

'I need a favour and I know you're the worst person to ask but...'

'Damn right I am!' Kyle said, puffing out his chest. 'No bribes. No favours. Nuffin.'

'...but I really need to see what was recovered from the *Penelope* crash,' Caleb finished.

Kyle McGinnis eyed him as though he wasn't just seeing the present moment Caleb but every Caleb stamped into every second of time: the good alongside the bad equally weighed. Caleb felt Kyle's appraisal like an eight year old would feel every nuance of expression on their parent's face as they internally wrestled to decide what to do to punish them for misbehaviour.

'As it happens I am in a bit of a fix,' Kyle said slowly. 'And that's rare for me, so pay attention. I didn't realise but Justin has tightened up security for this week, given our friends down from Command are here making themselves a pain in the neck whenever possible, and so I don't get to leave early to take my boy Jimmy home tonight like I planned. I've got a couple of people I could call but I'd rather do it myself. You reckon you could cover the last hour of the day? It's simple enough. No one in or out of records without a form signed by Justin and no one in or out of evidence without the same. If they claim it's urgent you can call me but otherwise tell them to fuck right off until they get that paper. Might be you could have a look at a few items undisturbed? Can't let you take it away though and if you breathe a word of it I'll get you fired.'

Caleb paused a moment. A warning light was flashing in his brain that made him think this could actually be a trap and it'd been a mistake to ask. Then again, he was fairly sure of his own ability to judge character. Kyle was a traditional man. If he trusted someone he was not a slave to bureaucratic process. At least that's what Caleb thought.

'So meet here at 4:30?'

Kyle smiled a crystalline but oddly cheerful smile.

'It's a deal Funeral Man.'

Caleb spent the rest of the day avoiding Justin and the auditors from Command while trying to find the officers who were there when Smiley escaped. After speaking to a few of his colleagues he found out there were two in today out of the dozens dispatched: Michael Delano and Jeffrey Portly. Both were PIs and had only been on the force 2 and 3 years. Caleb suspected the rest of the officers had been sent on leave in light of the auditors coming down. Justin would want to minimise the possible exposure.

This much was confirmed when he approached Michael Delano.

'Look, I already told you what happened,' he said, spotting Caleb walking towards him. 'It's not gunna sound any different the second time.'

'Wrong guy,' Caleb said, holding up his hands. 'Just got interviewed by them myself.'

Michael was short and had Hispanic features, with curly black hair and almond skin. He was meticulously clean shaven, though already had a five o'clock shadow. His build was solid, rooted; he stood with his arms folded as though no one in the world could push him over.

'Oh yeah? How'd it go?'

'I walked out on them.'

'Guess Justin's gunna chew you out later then huh?'

'I'll worry about that when later comes,' Caleb grinned.

The young man regarded Caleb for a moment.

'You're the dude they call the Funeral Man, aren't you? Working the Smiley case.'

Caleb nodded. Michael sighed.

'Look, I'm sorry we didn't get him. You gotta understand, it was like Murphy's Law: everything that could go wrong did. My grandmother would have called it the evil eye. I don't know if I share her beliefs but...' He shrugged.

'I'm not here to lay blame, don't worry. I just want to see if I can get a picture.'

Michael snorted.

'I'll give you a picture alright.'

He did, in great detail. What Caleb gleaned from the story was that they'd approached the wreckage expecting to find Smiley either dead or incapacitated but as soon as they had gotten within two hundred feet Smiley had opened fire on them with a heavy calibre weapon from the cover of the junker's wreckage, peppering Officer Chadwick with holes big enough to look through. They soon found themselves engaged in a fire-fight. Despite their best efforts no flanking attempts worked because the ship only had one entry point and Smiley's weapon was too high powered for them to approach any closer. Three more officers were shot dead and five more injured. Some would never walk again and had been discharged from service. When they finally got the opening to storm the junker, Smiley was gone and an empty SA101 lay on the deck.

They found the co pilot's body in the pilot room. Smiley crawled over twenty metres of broken glass and burning metal and then sprinted for the tree line with Eleanor Cole slung over his back. The officers had pursued and gone into the woods after him but soon lost him. This was where Michael Delano's description became something akin to a gothic scene.

'I'm not saying this is what happened,' he said. 'But it's what it felt like...'

He said it was as if there were other people in the forest, spirits, misleading and distracting him. Whenever he got on Smiley's trail or saw him in the distance he would trip up or else find himself running after one of his fellow officers.

Caleb had read all of this in the reports Justin had sent him while he returned to Earth on the GC, but hearing it from Michael's lips helped him to imagine it, to give it human colouring. It was no longer a series of events that didn't make sense. He felt Michael's panic, the disorientation. He could picture what the heavy thunder of the SA101 must have done to them: seeing Officer Chadwick shredded by the high calibre rounds.

He thanked Michael and went to find Jeffrey. Once he had the story from him his mental picture was even more complete. Their stories corroborated on almost every point except the final chase through the woods in which Jeffrey made no mention of spirits. He said Smiley disappeared as though he'd dropped through a trap door.

Later that day Kyle let him into the evidence locker. It was colourlessly illuminated by white glowing bars that left rainbow imprint on his retina if he looked at them too long. Rows and rows of shelves like the huge ceiling-scraper hardware store fixtures blocked view of the end of the room, making it feel more like a labyrinth. Kyle told him to wait and disappeared down of the labyrinth's many routes and returned with a waist high storage unit wheeled via a trolley-like device. Kyle detached the unit and hefted it up and put it down in front of Caleb with a gasp of relief.

Not bad for an old fella, he thought.

'Everything you need's here,' he said, patting the box.

'Nothing omitted. If even a fibre of hair isn't in there when I come back, I'm hauling your ass into early retirement. When you're done just put it back on the trolley and leave it there. Shut the door behind you and it will lock automatically.'

'Kapische.'

'Good man,' Kyle said. 'I'm off to pick up my boy.'

Kyle walked to the door. Caleb thought the interview was over when he heard Kyle growl back a comment, as though in passing.

'Catch this bastard will you, Funeral Man?'

When he looked up, Kyle was already out of the door.

He opened up the unit. There were only five items inside: an ornate cane damaged by fire, an old astronaut's helmet from the explorer days, magnetic boots, a tool box, and a medium sized box filled with technical components of the ship. By far the two items Caleb was most interested in were the helmet and cane.

He picked up the cane and looked it over. It had a silver wolf's head at its top and was made of refined polished wood now slightly dirtied by smoke and ash. He stroked the smooth surface, looking at the wolf head's intricate detail. He imagined he understood why people still went to antique shops and bought old tat now. There was something about holding an object from another era of human history that made one feel a deep connection to the human journey. No one regarded ornate items such as this as a status symbol anymore. Technology and credit count were the measure of wealth. But he imagined whoever had held this had felt a different kind of wealth.

He wracked his brains to think whether Smiley had ever mentioned a wolf in his pantheon but he couldn't recall it. It was unlikely to be his anyway unless he'd stolen it from someone at the Iron Caves. He suspected it belonged to the co pilot, unless Eleanor enjoyed gentlemen's finery.

As he was putting the cane back the wolf's head caught on the lip of the storage unit and pulled away to reveal a fine hidden blade. Caleb smiled. Not just for poetical reasons, then. He couldn't suppress the thought that he would have liked to have met Jim, the co pilot, but then he remembered he was dead. Smiley had beaten him half to hell and snapped his neck.

He sheathed the blade and put the cane back and then took out the helmet. 2K30 was printed on the side along with the initials S. P. The 2K30 mission was the first true human manned missions to explore Mars. What was one of them doing aboard Eleanor Cole's junker? Was it another one of Jim's relics? Somehow Caleb didn't think so. It was a clunky device, designed for practicality and to cope in various scenarios: as much for walking the Mars deserts and keeping out grit as for protection against cosmic rays when operating in space. He couldn't imagine Eleanor acquiring it from a dealer in the Iron Caves.

That left Smiley.

But how had Smiley gotten it? Caleb put his fingers to his temples and massaged. He needed a cigarette. A dull persistent ache ran through his forehead as though one of his veins was overburdened. His mouth was dry.

Smiley had to have obtained it after he escaped prison. There was no way they would have kept something like that at Facility 006. That brought him back to the dealer - but it still wasn't right.

'Tell me what deep, dark hole you found this in,' he said, staring at the black visor as though expecting a face to appear like some shimmering ghost on the other side.

It clicked.

It had been found in a deep, dark hole. The caves. The original owner must have lost it down there and Craig found it. That's how he had enough oxygen to stay down there: he potentially could have lasted days. The old black visor would also obscure his face unlike the clear rad-glass oxygen masks he'd seen the guards wearing. No one would bat an eyelid at him being secretive if guards were regularly going to the less reputable clubs in the Iron Caves.

There was more that this helmet could tell him. He knew it certain as he knew Martha waited for him on the other side; whatever doubts he sometimes had. He was hovering on the cusp of something, like a hawk levitating above the silhouette of its prey before it plummets and seizes it.

'Tell me,' he said. He turned the helmet round in his hands and saw the initials again: S.P. The names of the first explorers on Mars would be no secret. He could find them on the Internet and it was unlikely there would be two with the same initials. He pulled out his handheld and keyed in the initials though he wasn't likely to forget them, not with a hundred thousand volts of electricity running through him, not on the edge of the dive.

He returned the items to the box and locked the unit and replaced it on the trolley. It was much heavier than it looked and he admired Kyle's strength again. He fell into a coughing fit afterwards and cursed the day he first smoked a cigarette with his dad. He closed the security door and listened to it automatically lock behind him.

When he got home the first thing he did was sit down at his monitor and type in:

Mars 2K30 mission team

It returned a list of thirty to forty names, including the technical support units behind the ship, the navigation, and the mission planning. He typed in the initials and it narrowed the results to just one name.

Silvia Petrovich

He stared at that name and the accompanying profile link and picture for a good three minutes. The picture meant nothing to him. It showed a strong-featured Russian woman with short black hair wearing an old fashioned bulky astronaut's suit. The very helmet he'd seen in the evidence room was slung under one arm. She was handsome in her way; the features reminded him of a classical painting of Venus he'd once seen. He remembered being surprised at how attractive he found the old painter's unconventional portrayal of feminine beauty: a broad jaw, prominent nose, and angular chin. Silvia looked similar. He couldn't help but think all of that was very unimportant.

The name, however, had begun to add discomfort to his already pulsing head. The pain had relocated, moving from the throbbing vein in his temple to an ever-present ache at the back of his eyes that made him want to remove them. Where had he seen that name before and how did it connect to Smiley?

He dug out his old case files, slapped them down on his desk and began reading. He was still reading after the sky had grown dark and the city had turned radiant like the inside of a heated bulb. The pain in his eyes reached excruciating heights. He took ibuprofen, drank a glass of water and kept reading. Two hours later he realised he'd forgotten to eat as his stomach started producing stabbing pains, as though it was a parasite reminding him it needed feeding.

At last he gave up and went outside in the blue evening and smoked a cigarette and watched cars streaming by and relaxed as the warmth filled up his mouth. It reminded him of one of Martha's best kisses. He looked at the halogen night-lit Austin like the fantastical mirage of a real city. He wondered whether he was going crazy. He wished Tom was there to help him. For all Tom's faults he was rooted to Earth and a world that you could smell and taste and touch. Caleb felt adrift in space, but a space full of all the most terrible reflections, the echoing sounds of dead people and inescapable gods.

Shit, maybe I am going crazy.

Then for the second time that day he felt like a hundred thousand volts had just hit him.

He knew now exactly where he'd seen Silvia's name.

<>ACCESS LOGS</>
    <>AUSTIN POLICE DEP. TEXAS EARTH</>
    <>EXHIBIT NO. 11</>
    <>EXHIBIT FOUND IN SUSPECT'S APARTMENT AFTER ARREST</>
    <>BEGIN RECORD</>

> *seven kings and a bone-hewn crown*
> *a mouth that moves but makes no sound*
> *a light in which the darkness drowns*
> *a queen whose throne is in the ground*
> *a blade that rises like a mound*
> *an eye unblinking and unbound*
> *a mask that hides what can't be found*
> *worlds eons in the dying made young*

<>RECORD TERMINATES</>

Day 156

23RD May 2068

When Smiley woke it took him minutes to realise that he was still alive. His body was motionless and he could not move it. Was he paralysed? No. There was sensation. It'd started to creep back into his finger tips like a slow itch. There was weight. Terrible, terrible weight. A weight not even Atlas could have lifted. At least it seemed that way to the half conscious Smiley.

Sirens rang out. The fearful realisation he had run out of time crept upon him like someone pouring icy water down the back of his neck. He had only been out-cold a couple of seconds but that could be enough to cost his life and worse, cost the mission.

He struggled into a sitting position and felt like he tore his stomach muscles with just that simple action. His ears rang louder than the sirens. He touched his face and when he took his hand away there was blood. He ran his fingers over his face again and found his nose was crushed and misshapen. The old scars ached from the shards of glass that'd ravaged his face in the caves. It felt like a lifetime ago he'd knelt in supplication to the darkness and seen through the portal. He wished more than anything else a vision would come to him now, a vision to help him.

For a few precious seconds more he closed his eyes and prayed in silence. But there was only the sound of sirens. Only the pain. He smelled fire and smoke and having become aware of it choked and spluttered.

He tried to force himself up to his feet but collapsed again and lay flat, panting. The sirens grew louder and he forced himself up and tried again, this time standing fully. He felt a flush as though his circulation had lain dormant and now rushed into action. Dizziness swallowed his vision and he felt like someone spinning down a funnel that had no end point from which he could emerge. He almost collapsed again but stayed standing until it passed.

Captain Cole hung in the straps of the zero-g bed like someone crucified. Across the room the SA101 lay. He staggered over and bent to lift it. It slipped from his fingers and thumped on the floor as though magnetically attached. It was three times heavier.

'Fuck.'

He lifted the gun again and flung it over his shoulder like a heavy basket. He then staggered out through the security door onto the deck. It took him a few steps to realise the floor was tilted like a Fun House. Smoke poured from the engine room and he could see flames in the pilot room. Holding his breath, he made for the main door and then realised he'd forgotten his key-card.

'Fuck.'

He stumbled back. The junker's tipping floor almost betrayed him. The sirens were maddeningly loud. If he listened to them with concentration he thought they formed the words *LONNNNGGGG LIIIVVEEEEEEEE* over and over – but who did they praise? He screamed for the sirens to get out of his head. He grabbed the key-card off Captain Cole and ran back to the security door and pressed the key-card to the door and it rattled open.

He stepped outside and found himself standing in an open field. Over to the north and south there were endless strips of motorways. At his back, a forest stood like a dark army awaiting his command. Though a gleaming sunset illuminated the sky with rays of gold and yellow the pines remained dim and seemed to drink the light. Faceless, sharp and powerful they rose like megaliths erected by some unknowable people.

To the west, red and blue lights formed a jellyfish sea of shifting colour. They reminded him of the flashes seen through the smog of chemical clouds, of a war that had ended twenty years ago but was still raging in his mind.

A squad car swung horizontal and an officer ran out of it, pistol already in hand. He was shouting something to his colleague, but Smiley did not hear because his body was no longer under the control of his mind. It had been seized by his muscles.

He dropped to one knee behind a twisted piece of metal no doubt ripped from the bottom of the junker and let the wreckage take the weight of the machine gun. He had not had to think about where was best for cover. He knew it in the same way he knew this opponent was exactly two hundred and sixteen yards away and that the wind had dropped, though the latter didn't matter with the weapon he was carrying. In less than a second he cocked the gun and began firing. The officer nearest him was caught in a shredding burst and his shirt morphed from blue into red, like the lights on his squad car.

There was more shouting and more squad cars pulled up. The officers started taking cover behind their cars. Smiley gave them a sweeping arc of fire and felt the sweet, sweet recoil pounding his shoulder like a drill. Windows shattered and wheels burst. The heavy rounds ripped through the metal of the cars and forced the officers to crawl even further back.

He held them back like this for what felt like a day. The sun held a fixed position in the sky as though a spectator – breaking its constancy just to see the last of him. The long sunlight was a good thing: otherwise he would've lost sight of his enemies and they might have flanked him.

As it was, they were pinned.

They returned fire with shotguns, pistols, rifles but were always wide of the mark. Smiley was fully protected by the wreckage and out-ranged them.

One of the braver officers managed to crawl into a squad car and drove it full pelt towards him like something out of a *Mad Max* movie Smiley had watched when he was twelve. Smiley stood and unloaded a stream of fire through the windshield, killing the officer instantly. The four or five that'd tried to use it as cover to gain ground were left stranded in the open. He wasn't sure he killed all of them but they were out of the fight and some would never walk again.

At last, the sun dipped below the line of pines and the world turned from gold to a dark purple. The shadow cast by the forest looked to him like the dark mesh of a thorny crown. He saw other upright shadows of the officers skirting around the junker wreckage and realised he was about to find his fight coming to two fronts.

Staggering away from his cover, he kept offering pinning fire. He slipped through the security door. He found Captain Cole where he'd left her: unconscious. He threw the SA101 across the deck floor and drew out the army knife he'd stolen from Hank Marshall and began to cut her out of her straps. He did not have the strength to carry both the gun and her, so would have to take the risk.

She weighed 50 to 55 kilos, less than half the weight of the munitions packs he'd carried on his back all through Korea, but that had been a different time and he had been a young man.

He felt like he was bleeding on the inside.

Maybe he'd been shot?

He was covered in blood but he wasn't sure where it'd come from, so decided to go on. Captain Cole's limp body started to feel like the weight of the entire universe.

He reached the pilot room and stepped over Jim's body and then knelt by the shattered window and began shuffling on his knees over the broken glass. He could hear confused shouts and tramping footsteps. He didn't have far to go, just under the lip of the junker...

He emerged again onto the fields but this time closer to the pines. They were just twenty feet ahead. Though he knew they would pursue him he felt with frightening certainty if he crossed the line of the dark undergrowth they would not catch him, as though the forest was owned by a lord who would offer him asylum.

He rose to his feet. His knees felt as though his femur was crushing down on the bones in his lower leg and splitting them apart. His toes had gone numb and the underneath of his feet was so tightly cramped it was like walking on needles.

He ran on.

Gunshots followed him then he heard a commanding voice shout something and the gunshots stopped. Smiley felt some of the panic slide from him and a smirk twisted his features. The police killed random innocent people every day of the week – surely killing one more random innocent for the sake of putting the great Craig Smiley in the ground forever was worth it?

That was the thing about the world: it was so full of hypocrisy it had destroyed all mirrors capable of revealing the truth. It was the one thing about the liar Christ he could admire, he never stood for hypocrisy. Smiley thought of himself as the last of those mirrors that could show people what they really were. His master had been another but she was gone.

Gone but not forgotten, she said, close at his ear, the breath from her lips blowing onto the dwindling fire at his core and making it rise again. He leapt over a broken bough as though he was on Mars and unencumbered. Perhaps he could teach another? Maybe even Detective Rogers would come around, if his ignorance could be overcome.

You can overcome anything, his master said. *Because yours is not the strength of the world, it is the strength of so much more.*

But just as his elation rose to its zenith and he leapt another obstacle, another voice sent a jarring note like the blare of the sirens through his head.

Undiagnosed schizophrenia.

He stumbled and almost dropped Eleanor. He howled like an animal that does not understand where its pain is coming from.

He risked a glance over his shoulder and saw shapes moving through the trees after him, the lights of their torches like cyclopean eyes capable of burning his soul. Smiley plunged on, faltering with almost every step on the snaky, root-laden ground, but he somehow never fell. If he did they would catch him and that would be the end of the story.

Night took over the sky quick as sheet lightning. Smiley felt his breaths cold in his chest and the searchlights of his enemies were bright as pulsing beams shot from the armaments of spiritual beings. He thought he could also hear a jeep growling as it churned the woodland in pursuit of him like a boar of mythic stature. Three or four times he laid Eleanor down on the ground and lay on top of her and took a few moments of rasping, shaking rest. One time he did this he was fairly sure he blacked out for a few seconds and woke startled, dry-mouthed, fighting down a cough that felt like it was going to rip his throat. After that he grabbed Captain Cole and took stock of his surroundings and moved on and did not rest again. Somehow he was always either ahead or away from the lights despite exhaustion and the load he had to bear.

Once he came to within feet of a police officer and dropped Cole and slit his throat with his switch blade and watched him twitch on the floor as red vomit sprayed from his second mouth. They were all gateways, he thought. Every last being was a gateway trapping a greater soul behind its fleshly doors. One day even Smiley's would be freed. Perhaps it was even coming soon.

But not tonight.

As the night deepened the lidless searchlights faded until they became like wisps dancing between the trees, sprites that would lead a wanderer astray. The world of technology and metal slunk away and he heard the crickets pulsating hum like the congregation's drone. He heard the wolves sing hallelujahs. He heard the flap of muffled wings and the whole of life around and below and inside of him as though moving with one current and that current was the ebbing flow of creation that poured from the dark gateway. If he closed his eyes now he could see it.

Then the forest melted away, or rather, it melted into something new. The trees became slender, godlike creatures that marched alongside him as though answering a call. Cole's weight was lifted from his shoulders and he walked between the footsteps of the gargantuan beings. When he looked up there was no starlight only a darkness that moved over him like some great underbelly. Then he realised the slender creatures were not separate entities but the legs of some humungous spider crawling across the surface of the planet and he was filled with a terror so deep it almost stopped him in his tracks, but the memory of some natal fear drove him on and then he was once again stumbling through woods at night and the torches behind were vaguer and less real than stars.

He reached a clearing. He blinked as if to ward away the blackness but it only coiled into new shapes. He stared. Cole's weight incrementally returned and he sagged. He could not go much further. He was almost finished.

The clearing revealed its secret.

There was a cabin sitting in the midst of the dark forest that had no windows only walls and a bleak door and instantly he knew the cabin. He had seen it through the gateway. His heart moved up through his chest and into his throat and he swallowed down something that tasted acidic. He tried to breathe to quell the sickness he felt but his nose was filled with the stink of rotten wood. He fell to his knees and threw up over the moss and watched shining-backed insects crawl over his mess.

He let Cole slump down next to him against a tree-stump and looked at the hut. It did not seem real. He wasn't sure what he was waiting for. Maybe it was for the door to open and a figure to emerge with a crown of broken glass and eyes that knew so much.

The door did not open.

Open the Black Gate.

He went to the door and opened it and looked inside. It was nothing extraordinary. There were workman's tools on a table to the right of the door and an overall slung over a chair by the far wall. Boots caked in centuries of dust had been neatly placed underneath the chair. There was a small square trapdoor set in the middle of the floor and a doorless opening leading to a bedroom.

Instantly, Smiley knew that this was not the place.

It was the place and it wasn't the place.

It was the place he had seen in his vision in the caves of Mars: that much was certain. But it was not the place he needed to be. He was close. It was somewhere within these woods. But this was not the Black Gate.

His heart sank down from his mouth and into his stomach where it ached. He was always on the edge of knowing but never quite there, like someone trying to grasp the meaning of a dream. Sometimes he wondered whether he was dreaming. Other times he wondered whether he was insane just like the nurses and psychiatrists and wardens had told him so many times back in 46' when he'd been admitted. Well, they hadn't quite put it like that. They'd told him his mind created things.

'You feel, sometimes, like you are running through an unsolvable dream, yes?' the woman had said, the red dot on her forehead staring at Smiley with far more intensity than her white eyes below. Her bangles made soft noises like a dream-catcher as she spoke.

'Yes,' he'd croaked.

She nodded.

'This is what paranoia does: it sends the brain into a kind of loop. The paranoid latches onto something they believe to be the truth but because there is nothing truly to be found it creates evidence, tangential links.' She gave a soft chuckle and Smiley couldn't help but think of one of the weird sisters in a version of Macbeth he'd once seen: she'd given a laugh as though a person's sanity was of no consequence. It'd chilled him to his core then and it chilled him now. 'It is amusing that in small doses we consider this type of thinking as genius, but too much...well, leads to complications, shall we say. It makes life difficult.'

'Yes,' he'd said again.

'But we're going to make life less difficult for you.'

'Yes.' He paused. 'Thank you.'

That had been a moment he'd thought maybe he was sick and maybe it was possible to make the dark things at the corners of his mind and sight disappear. But after he'd shaken her hands and left the office he'd seen a strange old woman sitting in the corner. One that'd beckoned to him...

He shook himself and came back to the present in the dank hut. He went back outside and grabbed Eleanor and dragged her inside and shut the cabin door. He daren't light the hut though there were several matchboxes on the table and three oil lamps. Instead, he opened the trapdoor and peered down into the square of darkness. The excitement returned to him tenfold and he then couldn't resist fumbling with the matches until he lit one of the rusty lamps. There was a metal ladder underneath the table that he lowered into the opening and then climbed down, each step creaking as though he was a character in a stupid haunted house story.

There were no windows in the basements and the walls were made from grey mortar. As the light touched the corners of the room there was a second when he thought the emersion of that brightness would reveal a terrifying, curled form with a grin full of needle teeth, sitting in the room, waiting. But there was nothing except a few fetid looking rats huddled in the corner like squatters and spiders that moved disturbingly slowly across the walls as though brittled and half-dead. He kept his hand on the ladder at all times. He was frightened it would suddenly withdraw and he would be trapped. He climbed back up.

He pulled up the ladder and then lowered Cole through the trap-door and shut it over her and moved the heavy table over the trapdoor and sat in the corner of the room, at last letting go of consciousness with the same crazed relief of someone that'd spent days hugging a cliff face only to throw themselves into nothingness. He did not want to try the bed. He hadn't slept in a bed since 47' and he'd told himself that would be the last time.

He closed his eyes and thought he heard a low soothing *hushhh*. He ached to open his eyes to see which of the seven whispered him to sleep, but before he could he dropped into darkness and was lost amidst a carnival of sights he was sure he'd meant to forget.

DAY 170

Before she found what she found this morning everything was different.

For the last weeks (she was sure it had to be weeks though she had no measurement of time) the pain in her head had felt like a liquid filling up her skull to the very brim. Whichever way she lay or stood or sat it overwhelmed her. It grew like a monomaniac seed sprouting thorny roots that cut her brain as they pushed to reach the outside world.

Eventually, the pain had dulled, but did not go away. She knew she needed to see a doctor but there was no doctor here; she wasn't even sure whether she would ever see another human face again.

But then she had found the thing-that-changed-everything.

She'd found it scratching like a maddened fox at the ground until her hands bled; unearthing had been like unearthing the Grail. It might as well have been given wherever or whenever she was – she was starting to think she was dead.

She couldn't tell whether it was day or night only whether she was awake or asleep. Right now, she was awake and so was her captor: his footsteps groaned on the floor above. The walls might be made of mortar but the ceiling above was only wooden boards and damp, rotten ones at that which were sloughing away. Putrescent stalagmites hung around her. The rats giggled.

The croak of his footsteps moved above her and Eleanor was reminded of listening to the sound of thunder when she was a little girl: listening to the storm moving away.

Only this storm always came back.

Smiley disappeared for hours at a time. She assumed it was at first light but recently she'd started to wonder whether he went out by night and slept in the day so as to avoid being seen.

What he was doing was hard to determine. Her initial thought had been he was scavenging for food but he was gone too long and too often for that. It was something else. Perhaps he was looking for something. His gods. Whatever insane thing was inside his head. She'd no real idea. She guessed from the old floor boards and from a glimpse of a cabin room above that they were not in the city but she did not know where they were or whether the law was even looking for her. Jim was surely dead. Either her ship was in pieces or had been abandoned in some remote place.

Why hadn't Jim been able to do it? Why hadn't he just pulled the trigger?

Because he was a good man, she thought, and the ache in her head grew worse.

The biggest question of all was why she was still alive.

Smiley did not rape or torture her. That'd been her first fear when she'd seen the trapdoor open and garish light pour down through the opening. *He is coming,* she'd thought. *He is coming to molest you and do all the things in his sick head.* Instead, a sliver of half-cooked meat wrapped in yellow dock-leaf had fallen through the opening like manna. Then a bucket with fresh water in had been lowered by a skeletal arm. The trapdoor had quickly shut, leaving her in darkness. For a while she'd thought about starving herself, but then she'd crawled to where she thought it'd fallen and felt across the scummy ground until she found it. Her mouth had been inches from it when she felt a tickling across the back of her hand. Something large and many-legged was crawling across her food. She brushed it off and crawled into a corner of the room hyperventilating and finally bit into the meat, fighting the churning sensation in her belly. The meat tasted bloody and her belly went through a gauntlet of cramps for a few hours after eating it.

Having ruled out sick amusement and pleasure she wondered for the next few days (or at least, the next few meals) whether it was some kind of twisted pity that caused Smiley to keep her alive. If that was the case, however, she was sure he would have spoken to her by now. He was cold and clinical in the way he kept her; she didn't sense any willingness to connect. She'd expected endless sermons from him but she almost never heard him speaking except when he talked in his sleep. She would stand and press her ear against the filthy wooden boards and strain for a sound. What she heard made little sense to her other than confirming the idea he was going out of the cabin to comb the surrounding area in search of something.

Find it. Find it. Yes. Find it

No. No. Not again. Not again. Not again. No. No.

The mad yin-yang dialogue repeated itself night after night and sometimes went on for hours. Eleanor worried about her own sanity: sitting up listening to it when she could be thinking of a way to get out of her prison.

Whatever *it* was, he obviously hadn't found it yet. It could only be a good thing. If there was law enforcement out there looking for her then it was giving them more time. It was also giving her a chance to think of a way out.

So far all she had tried was digging but beneath the sludgy layer of earth she eventually met solid stone which she couldn't have gotten a spade through let along her bare hands. Digging through was no good.

But it was through the digging she found the-thing-that-changed-everything.

She listened hard for a repeat sound of footsteps but heard nothing except the rats.

This was it.

She already knew there was no lock on the trapdoor from the outside. Instead Smiley dragged a table or some other piece of furniture over it. In doing this he had either been careless or underestimated her.

Eleanor was used to carrying a 25kg sack of ore in each hand from a mine to her junker. Jim had used to joke she could win a dead-lift competition. She was small but not slight and certainly not weak. A few days ago when Smiley had been out she'd reached up and tried to push up the trapdoor but she was short by at least two feet.

And now she had the-thing-that-changed-everything that didn't matter.

Moving silently she skirted like a hunchback, clutching the-thing-that-changed-everything like a little girl's hand crossing a busy road. She stopped underneath the trapdoor.

She kissed the lead pipe and placed one end in the centre of the trap-door. The pipe was about ten feet long, long enough to push the door fully open. She bent her knees and got ready to shove. As she did so a shadow of the pain in her head emerged. *Not now*, she thought. She gritted her teeth. It throbbed like a living thing whose heart was restarting after hibernating. She bit her lip and fought down the growl of pain. Smiley was probably far out of hearing – in fact her plan depended on it – but she couldn't bring herself to let the sound escape. All she had to do was thrust it open with enough force that the table overturned and from there she could wedge the lead pipe in between and jump up. In theory it was simple. Lots of things were simple in theory. The metal was already slick in her hands.

She pushed.

Even though she was depleted and exhausted, she found it easy, but there was no way in hell she'd rush. With the care of someone lifting the lid of a jar found by the roadside she lifted the trapdoor. When she could see a couple of inches of the room through a thin slit she paused and moved around whilst keeping her lead pipe fixed, squinting to see the room above.

She continued to push up and there was a sound of creaking wood followed by a *shrrrieeekk* of metal scraping against something. Something thumped on the floor. The table must have tools on it, she thought.

Then she heard a second thump, more muffled than the last.

Shit.

She dropped the lead pipe and the trapdoor shut with a hiss like the noise *Penelope* made when the doors sealed and became airtight. She stood holding her breath staring up at the door. She heard another door creak open. Footsteps. They paused over her. A scratching noise almost made her scream and then she realised it was Smiley picking up whatever tool had fallen off the table. She almost thought she could picture him turning it over in his hands.

Two footsteps. A light tapping. What was he looking at now?

Eleanor couldn't get it out of her head that if he found her with the pipe that would be her only means of escape gone and then she was fucked. Completely fucked.

The footsteps retreated and she heard the door open and close. *But no further footsteps.* He was playing a game with her now. Testing her. Seeing if she tried again.

She waited – perhaps half because she couldn't move. A kind of dream-paralysis had overcome her entire body and her skin was coated with clammy sweat. The feeling that if she moved everything would collapse around her was irrepressible.

Then he spoke.

'It must be lonely down there, Captain Cole. I know what it's like. I was imprisoned once too. You feel as though your world has shrunk and your spirit has shrunk with it. You ask yourself the question as to whether a soul can be beaten out of you like imperfections out of metal.'

She lay down the pipe and put her hands over her ears. She wasn't listening. She couldn't. Not to him. *He killed Jim.*

'There were days when I wanted to kill myself,' he went on. 'There were days where I dreamed of escaping. Those dreams were always crushed.'

The footsteps started up again only this time rapid, urgent. She couldn't get the image of a pacing tiger out of her head.

'You must be feeling those things now. You must want to get out. But let me tell you a secret Captain Cole. Getting out will get you nowhere. Do you want to know why?'

He waited a few seconds for her answer. She thought she heard a soft chuckle.

'The prison you are in is not made of mortar and earth. It's in your *head.* That's where our real imprisonment takes place. We imprison ourselves. We are imprisoned by society and its rules. The physical prison only serves to remind us of his fact and make us aware we are trapped.'

This was what she had anticipated all along: these awful toxic words that fell on the weakened resistance of her mind like acid. The rooted ache spread its thorny limbs and she crouched and clutched her head with the pain.

'You think you are desperate after two weeks?' The voice had risen to a growl now and the pacing got more frantic. 'I was inside for *seven years.* Seven years! What I could have done in that time! What I could have achieved!'

The footsteps stopped abruptly, as though the batteries animating the stomping thing had died. She heard heavy breathing and couldn't tell whether it was her own or his.

'Don't try to escape, Captain Cole,' he said. His voice was treacly: she couldn't tell whether it was with emotion or something else.

The footsteps retreated into silence.

Eleanor breathed for what felt like the first time in minutes. It was as if she had stood under the paralysing gaze of some terrible monster and only now the gaze moved on and she was free again. She would not try again today. She wasn't sure if she would try again at all.

'Pull yourself together,' she said, quietly. 'He's just trying to scare you.'

And it'd worked. Without Jim to back her up she felt powerless against him. Maybe Jim wasn't dead? Maybe he was captive in another cellar just like this one? Maybe he'd gotten away from the crash while Eleanor was unconscious.

The suggestions sounded weak even in her head. She could *feel* that Jim was dead, as though he'd been a twin brother. He'd warned her against taking the offer. He'd *known* deep down. But she'd been thinking about money, about her life, about starting to get tired of scraping a living off transporting rocks around. She'd been thinking about a lot of things she probably should have talked to Jim about because he would have had some solution. He was always good with solutions – even if it was just making her laugh.

All the anger she felt for Smiley flipped and turned inward, driving like real knives into her body. The pain in her head exploded and she felt as though the roots were now so deep they could never be dislodged. *I am to blame. I am to blame.* You had a ship. You had a crew. You let them down.

And then she cried. She cried like she had done as a little girl afraid of the thunder.

A noise made her start up. The trapdoor was open. A ladder descended through it. Someone was coming down. She raised the lead pipe and sank into as best a stance as she could, keeping the pipe poised in front of her like a spear. But it wasn't Smiley. It was a man in a white accountant's shirt, bespectacled, holding a book.

It was her father.

He didn't say anything at first. He did not even greet her. All he offered was the warmest smile she knew. Every hair on her body stood on end. He looked fuller, more substantial, more colourful than any memory of him. He was realer than reality, far realer than the grey four walls in which she was imprisoned. She experienced a sensation she had never felt before – the opposite of falling into a dream. She had the feeling that her whole life had been one long sleep and now she had *woken up.* That feeling terrified her more than she could say.

'Dad?'

'Hello Ellie.'

'Why...what..'

He put a finger to his lips.

'We need to talk quietly.' He pointed to the ceiling. That was enough. He came towards her and sat down next to her, cross-legged like a schoolboy just like he had done in life.

She sat next to him.

'Why are you here?' she whispered.

'To help you, of course,' he said, as though there was nothing strange about the fact he could be here, even when Eleanor had watched him die.

He held up the book. It was *The Odyssey,* the exact same copy he used to read her when she was little with the crease mark on the front cover from where he used to bend it around the back while reading. Her mother always told him off for that. *It damages the spine,* she'd say, with a finger-wag.

'Do you know where you are?' he said.

She shook her head.

Her father only smiled.

'Yes you do.' He opened the book. 'You are in the cave of the Cyclops.'

Eleanor blinked. She hadn't thought it possible but the feeling of waking from the longest sleep imaginable grew on her. What was this?

'Dad...'

'And do you remember how Odysseus escapes?'

She forced herself to remember.

'He ties himself under the sheep. When the Cyclops lets them out they slip out.'

Her father nodded.

'But before that, he blinds the Cyclops, doesn't he? If the Cyclops could see Odysseus tied under the sheep, it would never have worked.'

'So, I have to blind Smiley?'

'Or wait until he is blinded,' her father said. 'Patience, as much as anything, sees Odysseus through.'

Her father stood.

'I have to go now.'

'Wait!'

But he was already gone. He had always been gone. The room was as dark and empty as it had ever been.

<>ACCESS LOGS</>
   <>PSYCHOLOGICAL CLINIC AUSTIN POLICE DEP. TEXAS EARTH</>
   <>RECORD NO. 661</>
   <>CREATED 09:45:33 25/10/2058 EARTH TIME</>
   <>BEGIN RECORD</>

THERE ARE two types of people in this world: those whose bodies die first and those whose minds die first.

There are more people of whom the latter is true than you think. In fact, there are billions of them walking around right now.

No. Smiley never said this. I'm saying it.

I need a cigarette.

<>RECORD SUSPENDED</>

DAY 239

'Tom, I have a lead.'

Caleb sat on his bed after the first good night's sleep he'd had in eight years. Daylight was just beginning to probe the darkened room and for once the long shadows it cast did not alarm him and he did not worry that they would take shape. In the night he'd woken once and gone to the toilet and on his way back had stopped in surprise realising he hadn't seen the dead girl once.

'Whass that?'

Drunk. Again.

The anger Caleb felt was almost enough to make him hang up, but he was prepared to give Tom another chance.

'I have a lead. It's a woman committed to the same institution as Smiley. Silvia Petrovich.'

'The explorer who lost her helmet?'

'That's the one.'

When Caleb had searched up the helmet there had been half a hundred results. Most of them were extracts from small side columns in newspapers. They mentioned the tiny detail that one of the astronauts had lost their helmet while exploring the caves but had been unharmed as a sidebar - nothing more than a fun fact for the day. Caleb certainly hadn't remembered it, and he was a repository of facts. When he used to go to the pub quizzes on holiday in England with Martha he became something of a local sensation.

But those were days from another life: Caleb had to think about now. Though it'd just been an anecdote in the papers thirty-odd years ago now it was the cornerstone of Caleb's theory. He wasn't sure whether this theory would explain where Smiley was now but it couldn't hurt given where the search teams were.

'Whythefuck should I care about that?'

'Because...'

'Whythefuck should I care about any of it, in fact?' Tom roared over him. 'I fucking *hate* my job. I don't know why I kept fucking doing it all those years. Maybe 'cuz I kidded myself I was good at it? Maybe 'cos Justin upped my pay every time he thought I was gunna jump ship. I don't know. I wish I fucking had...wish I'd spent more time with Melinda.'

Then Caleb realised what'd happened. This was nothing to do with the case. He'd told Melinda.

'Why'd you tell her man?'

There was a pause and all Caleb could hear was an awkward glugging sound.

'I guess... after Smiley...' He choked.

Caleb could finish the sentence: *After Smiley called you out in front of me, your boss and half a hundred colleagues you couldn't take lying to her anymore.*

'That's what he does,' Caleb said. 'He messes with your head.'

'It wasn't him,' Tom said, perhaps a little too quickly. 'It's me. I was wrong. He's not the cause of all the world's evil, Cal. It's the system. The system's broken...'

'It's only broken if you let it break,' Caleb said, feeling himself growing hot under the collar. Suddenly the sunrise seemed a vicious red through the blinds.

'I didn't fucking let it break, you fuck, it was broken long before we ever joined the force!'

'You're no better than a kid saying "it was like that when I got here",' Caleb said, more venom in his voice than he'd intended. But how could anyone be so childish now? 'What the hell happened to you? One thing goes wrong and you just fall over?'

'It ain't one thing, it's *every*thing man. How long we been fucking doing this? All the shit we've seen. All the shit we've *done*. Fuck me, you might think you're buying yourself some ticket to heaven putting Smiley away but I know better...it's all fucked man...'

'Look,' Caleb said, forcing his voice into an even tone. 'All I know is we came through. Time after time. Through the roughest shit. If you don't think that's God then I'm fine with that, but at least have some fucking perspective.'

'And where's your God now, eh?'

For a second, Caleb thought he heard a different voice on the end of the line, a voice that created static, a voice that spoke in lulling paradoxes, a voice he *hated*. He pulled the handheld away from himself and stared at it for a moment and shivered all over and then pushed the ludicrous idea out of his head. That's exactly what Smiley wanted him to think: that he could do things like that.

'Eh?' Tom pursued. 'Where is he? Smiley's still out there. No matter how many times we catch up to him he always gets away. Prison. The crash landing. Hell, let's go back a little further: a fucking war, the psych ward. If your God's real he's doing plenty to keep him alive. I'm starting to think his...'

Caleb ended the call and threw his phone across the room as hard as he could and yelled at the top of his lungs.

Fuck Tom.

He'd do it himself.

Two hours later Caleb stood outside the Austin Military Hospital, a towering white columned building evidently designed to resemble the Parthenon but without any of its artistic qualities. The white marble was bare and unadorned. The rows of square windows looked like surgical incisions in the stone. Caleb wondered how anyone could think something as ugly as this could be good for someone's mind.

Inside, the building was far more modern and even uglier. The sickening combination of over-hygienically treated surfaces with unhygienic people produced an acidic taste in his mouth. Everything was green and looked plastic: the floor, the walls. He wondered whether it was supposed to recreate the peace of an outdoor scene. If it was, it was a miserable failure.

There was a team of three or four nurses chatting in the lobby; one of them broke away and made their way towards him. Behind the nurses stood a door with a small window through which he spied a common-room. A group of patients in overalls were sitting around in huddles that reminded him of cowherds. From the way they moved they looked as though they were sleepwalking.

'Can I help you?' the nurse asked in a way that suggested she would rather throw him out of the door.

'You can, actually,' Caleb said. He flashed his badge. He noticed the instant straitening of her back, a posture alteration that often indicated wariness. Caleb was not a power-freak but he had to admit it felt damn good. 'Caleb Rogers from the Austin Police Department. There was a patient here a while back. She was admitted sometime in 2040 I believe. Silvia Petrovich.'

The nurse nodded.

'Charlie!'

One of the nurses turned and made her way over, concealing a grimace rather poorly.

'This Detective...Rogers?' She shot a questioning glance. Caleb nodded.

Charlie looked distrustful to say the least.

'He just needs to know about Silvia Petrovich,' the first nurse said soothingly. Caleb wondered whether she talked to her patients the same way. Charlie cleared her throat.

'She was here. Terrible shame after everything she did for this country. She used to tell the most fascinating stories when she was lucid. Silvia suffered from terrible panic attacks. She must have suffered some trauma out there when she was on Mars because she was very frightened of wide open spaces. I think it reminded her of the great emptiness of space, you know? It's hard to imagine what it's like. I've never been off planet.'

Caleb sucked it all in like a sponge.

'I have. It is scary even now when there are colonies. I can't imagine what it was like when there was hardly anything to go to. Just empty buildings built by machines.' The first nurse looked at him with something like awe. Charlie looked less impressed. There was a girlish quality about her face though it wasn't what he would define as typically attractive. She had pretty blonde hair. She looked young, far too young to remember Silvia. He said as much to her and she blushed crimson.

'I'm actually turning 51 this year. I started here the year before Silvia was admitted.' She touched her hair. 'This is dyed.' She sighed. From that single gesture Caleb unravelled a whole story of a woman whose looks had never been acknowledged by anyone ever. Caleb's comment came thirty years too late. 'Anyway, enough of that,' she said. 'Why are you asking about her?'

'There was another patient here,' Caleb said. 'He was admitted later. In 46.'

Her face fell and he knew she knew who he meant.

'Smiley.'

Caleb nodded.

'He's been on the news lately,' the first nurse chimed. 'First Mars and now this. Do you think they'll find him?'

Justin Walker had been against letting out the news Smiley was back on earth. Caleb had pointed out there were over two hundred videos of the crash landing posted on the web within three minutes of it happening. No cover up was going to fly. Besides, Caleb thought it good to make people a little warier. A widespread panic was unlikely given it was only a single convict and not a natural disaster.

'That's why I'm here,' he said, as a half truth.

'You think he's...' she looked around.

'No. No. Not at all. However, I think there might be a clue to where he is now here.'

'What do you mean?'

'Did Smiley ever speak to Silvia Petrovich?'

Charlie pulled a face and rolled her eyes into the top of her head as through trying to see what was inside her brain.

'Yes, actually. They sat together quite a lot. It was like they had a weird connection. I always thought it was because, well, they'd both had traumas, hadn't they?'

Yes, Caleb thought, they certainly both had that.

'Though they were also very different,' she went on. 'Silvia was a meticulous planner. She would tell us everything she was going to achieve that day right down to every detail, even though some of it was fantasy. Smiley was just – he just responded to the moment. An opportunist. Any lapse he'd miss his pills or slip from his room...'

And then, as she was talking, Caleb realised he was an idiot. She had just spotted something he had not spotted in nine years, or rather, she had put into words something he'd been trying to grasp.

An opportunist.

Craig Smiley was not a planner. He might have an ultimate aim but he did not have a master scheme to get there. He was responding to each thing as it came and overcoming it, making the best with what he had, exactly as he'd been trained to do. He was not an officer. He had never been a strategist. He was a grunt who was thrown into the shit and had to deal with it or die.

That was how he escaped the prison.

That was how he got out of the firefight.

That was what he was doing now. Making do. He was not sitting in some bunker he had spent years preparing. He was running through the woods waiting for the gunfire to stop and the search parties to go away so he could regroup and push on.

To beat him, all they had to do was think ahead.

But how?

As if in answer to his thoughts his handheld started ringing. He excused himself and walked outside and answered.

'Caleb.'

'Where are you?' It was Justin and he had that tone of command again which made Caleb's gut wrench.

'I'm sorry Chief: I was just running up a few leads.'

'It doesn't matter. Get here. Now.'

Caleb sighed.

'The other day, with the auditors, I...'

'Fuck the auditors; they found her Caleb. They found Eleanor Cole.'

The world became a vacuum around him. There was no sound other than the metronome of his heartbeat very softly and very slow at the centre of it. He could hardly breathe.

'Caleb, she's alive.'

<>ACCESS LOGS</>
  <>PSYCHOLOGICAL CLINIC AUSTIN POLICE DEP. TEXAS EARTH</>
    <>RECORD NO. 662</>
    <>CREATED 09:55:14 06/11/2058 EARTH TIME</>
    <>BEGIN RECORD</>

PEOPLE THINK that madness comes in one fell swoop.

That's fucking ridiculous.

Madness comes at a gradual creep. Imagine you are a sculpture. Every day a small metal file is taken to you and a little is scraped away. The next day a little more is taken. Millimetres. One day someone will step back and look at the statue and realise it is not the same. The essential nature of it has altered. Its *meaning* has changed. Even its purpose.

But until that day, all you feel is a slow grating. Not enough to make you do anything but just enough to for you to know something is wrong.

I've heard cops boast about whether they were there when Mike Saunders 'lost it' and brought a shotgun into the APD and started capping but they're talking bullshit. Everyone was there when he lost it. Everyone was there every day helping it happen. People think that because they work in the same building as someone for a few months they know them.

Shit, half of the people I meet don't even know themselves.

The other half know a little and are making the rest up. I don't think I know Tom and he's supposed to be my damn partner. He could screw me over in a few years time. Who knows?

There's this passage in Revelations I love that says every person will be given a stone with their true name engraved on it but they won't recognise the name. I think that's a metaphor for what I'm saying: no one knows anyone except God, and he's keeping it a secret.

Well, at least til' Judgement Day.

<>RECORDED SUSPENDED</>

DAY 238

Eleanor lay like someone catatonic, staring up at the ceiling and listening to the heavy footsteps on the floor above. She followed them as they shuffled from her left to the right. She anticipated the sound of the creaking door opening and shutting.

She inhaled and held the breath in her chest without consciously wishing to do so.

The footsteps meandered back to the left.

He always does food first, remember.

The trapdoor opened. A limp piece of meat fell through the opening. The trapdoor shut.

She let out her breath, deflated.

Eleanor was not someone accustomed to waiting or to patience. She forced herself through it now because she *had* to, because she was sure that regardless whether or not she was crazy and seeing things it was her only way of escaping.

She had almost never had to wait for anything in her life. If she wanted a good time she went down to the Rock Biter and walked up to the bar and got talking and before the hour was up they'd be back in her junker with her riding him like a prized bull. If she wanted money she went out to the miners and told them she needed cargo and that was that. Waiting killed her. Maybe that'd been what led her to be stupid enough to take Smiley's fake job in the first place.

But now she had a reason to wait.

She'd tried to escape twice more since her first attempt. Both times no sooner had she levered open the trapdoor than she heard footsteps. It was like Smiley was summoned by opening it. Maybe he never went as far as she thought. She couldn't know for sure. The last time she'd tried she had been half way out of the trapdoor and had to throw herself back down, twisting her ankle. It'd taken weeks for her to recover. All that time she spent cursing herself for being so impatient.

But the twisted ankle had forced her to stay still, to think. And this thinking had brought on a realisation.

Smiley was spending longer and longer out on his searches.

The Cyclops was losing his vision, but he was not blind yet.

Eleanor knew she had to be cautious. Whatever the reason he'd kept her alive she was sure she was not indispensible. She'd had to test her theory. Given she had no accurate measure of time it was not easy. At first she'd tried counting the seconds but that proved impossible. No one could count for hours and not go mad with it.

There was no light in the chamber to make a makeshift sundial. There was no way she could see the outside world.

But two days ago she'd found another way to calculate the time. She'd spilled some of the water from her daily bucket to see if anything would come to drink from it. The rats periodically scoured the dank basement. She wondered whether it was for water.

When they found the puddle she'd created their squeaks of excitement rang through the basement like a parody of joy; they suckled at the puddle as though it was a breast. After that they returned to it every few hours until there was no water left.

Eleanor refilled it. She was careful not to give too much. She knew she needed to remain hydrated to survive. Just enough to test her theory. The rats returned. This time she measured them against Smiley.

At first, the rats had been drinking two or three times in the space between him leaving and returning. Now it was more like four.

The footsteps moved from left to right again and she breathed.

The door whined on its hinges and then clicked shut.

She began counting. Each count she visualised one of his loping footsteps. He had to be a good distance from the hut before she could move. He was not at his peak anymore but probably still in better condition than her and taller.

When she had counted four minutes out she stood and grabbed the lead pipe and stood under the trapdoor and placed the pipe on its underneath. With one thrust she flung it open and there was a crashing noise as the table overturned.

No time for caution now. This was *it*.

She jumped and caught onto the trapdoor ledge and hauled herself over the lip, surprised by just how difficult it was. Her forearms shook. The lead pipe slipped from her grip and clattered below.

There was no way in hell she'd go back for it now.

Come on, don't fuck it up now.

She rolled over the edge and struggled to her feet. The hut was entirely windowless and dark. From what her eyes could see (they had become accustomed to darkness) it was small and mean and dirty. The tools were ugly and badly kept. Drums of a toxic looking substance stood in one corner of the room. Her urge was to fling herself out of the front door and run into the wilderness but she knew she needed to buy herself some time.

She shut the trapdoor and pulled the table upright. She replaced the table on top of the trapdoor and then began piling the tools randomly onto the table again.

A snapping twig made her leap out of her skin and almost scream. She ran for the door and burst through it and saw the silver silhouette of a deer scarper away like a soul speeding from its body. The stars hung overhead but there was no other light to be seen. She had half expected to come nose to nose with Smiley, his face lit by an orange light that suggested torn volcanic earth.

But it was just an animal. Not him.

Shut the fucking door, idiot.

She ran back and shut the door to the hut and then sprinted off into the wilderness hoping against all hope she wouldn't meet him in the woods now.

Like a naked wild creature of a primordial Earth she leapt and ran through the woodland. The longer she ran the faster she ran. Her legs were sore and wooden, unused to being stretched, but the fear that'd been locked away inside her head and heart was finally being allowed to sweat out of her like a toxin and she could not stop the mad rush taking her over.

On and on she ran.

Every hiss or rustle or snap spurred her; her sense told her she was free but everything else told her the entire forest was one dark entity and that entity was Smiley and each shadow was a limb seeking to snare her.

When she glanced back over her shoulder, she was sure she would see him bearing down on her, grinning, whispering.

The shadows grew. She started to lose vision: everything was a closing tunnel. Then she knew he *was* behind her. She couldn't turn her head for fear. He followed like a dream-stalker and no matter how fast she ran her legs would never carry her fast enough.

The evening stretched like a nightmare caught in the endless cycle.

Purple bloomed like a flower of the underworld and she realised she'd run all through the night. She turned. There was no one behind her.

God she was tired.

Thinking it meant she could not go any further, as though her body would have been able to carry on if her mind hadn't woken to reality. She slid down next to a fallen pine and lay there with a mouth as dry as the sands of Mars and nothing in her head except a fear of him catching up to her and exhaustion like no other. All sense of who she was left her at that moment. There was only living and the prospect of relief or death and the prospect of relief.

She fell asleep before she had time to think she couldn't.

DAY 239

She woke to the sound of birds and warmth on her face. How long had she been without sunlight down in the basement? It was life-giving and she understood why once older cultures had knelt under the sun's rays and worshipped it.

She wanted to lie under the warmth of that sun and listen to the sounds of the birds forever but she knew that would be dangerous. That would invite the wolf to find her scent again.

She stood and began walking. The dryness in her mouth had only gotten worse. Her stomach didn't growl with hunger. The crude, half-cooked meals had curbed her appetite. When she looked down she saw there was barely any shape to her body now. She was stick thing. *Like him.* The thought made her shudder. Every muscle in her legs protested.

The trees thinned. Then they morphed. They became slender cypresses, like the colonnades to a temple. Then they stopped altogether. She stood at the edge of a vast plain coloured auburn and gold with sunlight like the mane of some colossal lion that slept eternally. It was one of the most breathtaking things she had ever seen and she had seen the stars in naked glory.

Birds swooped low over twisting rivulets of clear water that wormed docile paths through the long grass. She ran to the water's edge. A troop of mottled ducks squawked complainingly at her as she splashed the cold water on her face. Then she crouched by the water and debated whether it was worth risking a drink. She was parched and felt like the sun might kill her without the shade of the canopy. What more could a parasite do to her?

She scooped cupfuls up to her mouth and her body shuddered as the water went down. She realised it'd been a long time since she'd tasted water that hadn't been pasteurised and chemically cleaned. They could colonise Mars all they wanted but it would never have this.

She stood, feeling better, and decided to follow the little river. She soon found it gave way into something much bigger and the area around it was submerged at least knee deep though it didn't look it because of the long grass. She trudged on. She only had ugly pilot's boots on anyway and she couldn't worry about looks now: she probably looked like a ghost. She laughed. A great egret gave her a curious look before continued to stalk through the marsh keeping a yellow eye turned on the waters for sight of any prey it could snatch up in its overlong beak.

A few hundred metres up the river she saw a dead bird torn apart in the shadow part of the water, mud curling around its body. It looked rotten. She tried not to think about it.

After the bird Eleanor spotted an alligator lying by the side of the waters, almost indistinguishable from the grey depths except for the gnarly lumps on its back and the hint of scales. She made a sharp turn and moved away, circling around it. The alligator didn't seem that interested however. Maybe it had just eaten.

She came upon drier land. How far had she walked? She felt it must be miles. She looked back at the line of the cypresses. Four? Five? She cupped her hand to her brow to shade her from the sun. There was a dark spot hovering above the trees. She squinted. Her eyesight had been near perfect when she first started as a junker but after months in the basement they felt dulled. They hurt at the centre when she strained to see detail. The spot was not a craft or a plane. It was an ibis, and it wasn't dark, its colour transmuted as it moved like a living rainbow:

turquoise, purple, red, blue. The sight filled her with awe and dread. The latter perhaps came from some kind of dim association in her brain with the ancient Egyptian gods. They were too close to the dark things Smiley talked about.

Suddenly she became afraid of how easily she could be seen standing out in the open. She crouched down.

'No point hiding now.'

Her heart froze and she turned. The ground beneath her was wet and she slipped, falling flat on her back. She tried to scramble to her feet.

'Easy there.'

She looked at where the voice was coming from. There was a man standing not far off wearing a brown uniform and with even browner skin showing beneath his peaked cap and short sleeves. It was the kind of skin a medieval farmer might have had. There was a yellow and black badge on his arm sleeve and he looked concerned.

'Who are you?' she said.

The man laughed.

'I was about to ask you the same question, missy. Are you lost?'

'Yes,' she said. It couldn't be denied at this stage.

The man nodded.

'Not to worry. Good job I found you before you accidentally pissed off a gator, if you'll pardon the phrase.' He took off his hat like a poor man out of an old western film and placed it over his heart. 'Name's Daniel Cooper. I work with Anahuac National Wildlife Refuge. You must have walked a long way to get lost here.'

She stood, unsure whether she was about to wake up. The word *refuge* rang in her ears as though he'd bellowed it.

'You've no idea.'

He laughed.

'Look like you've got quite a story to tell.'

He eyed her up and down, but not in a lascivious way. It was the kind of appraisal Jim might have given her after she came back from a hard day arguing with the miners, a look that was actually to see where she was emotionally. It was what made Jim so much better than half the straight men out there. He actually fucking *looked*.

She was still aware that it would be foolish to trust Daniel Cooper on that premise alone, however. She'd gotten this far, it paid to stay cautious just a little longer. It reminded her of the last few feet of descent when landing a junker. Sure, you were probably home dry when it came to the last ten feet, but did you really want to risk it and tear out your hull?

'What's your name miss?'

'Eleanor,' she said, after a while. 'Eleanor Cole.'

Daniel's jaw dropped.

'Holy Jesus.' He coughed and replaced his hat. 'Pardon mam, it's just...well... we've been looking for you.'

'You have?'

'Yeah, it was your junker crashed out of the sky couple of months back, wadn't it? Jesus! We thought we'd never find you.'

Eleanor could feel herself shaking. She was sure this could not be real. The only thing better would be news they'd found and shot Smiley a few hours before they found her.

'Neither did I.'

Daniel chuckled again.

'My truck is a few hundred metres yonder. I can take you back to the reserve and from there the police will come and pick you up. There's plenty of rangers around so you'll be just fine.'

She nodded. No, she thought, she wouldn't be fine. She could be alive. She could even be healthy. But she could not be fine for a good long while.

But she could think about that later.

'Sure,' she said as though reaffirming what she'd agreed to and she walked over to the ranger.

She walked like a somnambulist until she could see the gleaming white truck up ahead. Daniel talked non-stop the whole way. She tried to focus on what he was saying but it was impossible, her thoughts were rabid.

Her stomach also hurt a great deal. It wasn't just cramps like she normally got. This was different. It felt as though a stone had gotten caught in her intestines and they were trying to squeeze it out. She wanted to shit all of a sudden – no, she *needed* to shit. It was like there was an itch in her bowels that could only be scratched by letting it go.

'Daniel, I...'

But then the uncomfortable stone became a solid ball of pain. She collapsed as though someone had pulled a plug out of her. She didn't feel any impact. She was unconscious before she hit the sodden earth.

Between the instant descent of darkness and waking up to blaring, angry light, there wasn't much she could accurately remember. Sound remained the only constant throughout the absent space as though her ears had continued to record everything even when everything else shut down. She recalled radio static, an engine growling like a deep-throated beast, urgent voices: some of them were familiar and some very alien. At one point all sounds gave way to the squeak of an overused wheel spinning and spinning; it stretched across the dark canvas like an everlasting brushstroke. She was sure it would never end. It would spin on even after human life was extinguished: the last machine left on Earth that'd never been shut off. At one point she thought it was not a wheel but mice sniffling as they searched along a dank wall for water.

The things that she did see interrupted the darkness like sheet lightning did the night sky. The images, or rather, her experience of them, did not seem bound by the experience of time. Like a slideshow she could drift backwards and forwards through them.

She saw a wild yellow wasteland spinning around her as though she was tied to the heart of a spinning wheel. A mask descended over her face, a mask that was not a mask but an oxygen breather.

A masked face hovered near her own as she heaved her own guts into a bowl over and over again and cried like a beaten school-child and prayed to as god she wasn't sure existed that it would end. Soothing, empty words came out of the masked face.

Apparently it would all be over soon.

The next patch of darkness was broken by a wraith-thin man standing at the end of her bed, paralysing her like the man with the brimmed hat she'd been haunted by as a little girl. He was dressed all in black as if attending her funeral. *Smiley. Smiley was there.* No! She screamed.

A dream. A fantasy of escape. She would wake to find out she was dying in the basement and Smiley would be with her at the end to take her soul into his awful world.

Then there was angry light and waking.

Dull pain.

She blinked.

It took her a long time to realise she was lying in a hospital bed and her arm was hooked up to a saline drip. She coughed, phlegm blocking her windpipe. She blinked again.

A nurse stood by her bedside changing over her saline drip. When she saw Eleanor was awake she turned and smiled. She had elegant Spanish features and hair that glistened like silk even bunned up. Eleanor couldn't help but think waking to a face like that was wasted on her.

'Good to see you awake, Captain Cole.'

'What...' She coughed. The nurse didn't wait for her to try again.

'You had a water parasite. Cryptosporidium.'

Eleanor nodded.

'How long was I out?' It felt like weeks.

'Only a few hours. The ranger who picked you up this morning dropped you off at 10:00. It's 17:00 now.'

She nodded again, though she wasn't really sure she understood anything.

'How did it hit me so quickly?'

The nurse frowned.

'What do you mean?'

'It...I...It was the river I drank from this morning, right? There was a dead animal in it... It...'

'Cryptosporidium takes two to three days to manifest symptoms so you got it way before then. It must have been somewhere else. You make a habit of drinking from rivers?'

Eleanor would normally have thrown back a retort but she was too tired.

'I guess so.'

Natural water wasn't all it was cracked up to be.

'Your immune system was heavily compromised,' the nurse said. 'It made it worse than it normally is. You may have to stay in the hospital for the next couple of weeks. Other than that, no harm done.' The nurse smiled. 'I should let you know you have a visitor. He's been waiting for you to wake up. Would you like to see him?'

Him. There was only one *him* she knew who would visit her. She didn't think for a second it might be Smiley – he'd become a distant thought already, a shadow in her past that she'd moved on from. Her heart leapt in her chest.

'Please,' she said, forcing a smile. The nurse nodded and shuffled off, drawing the curtains around Eleanor's bed to give her some privacy. A few moments later the curtains parted and Eleanor pushed herself up on her elbows.

'Where the fuck have you been?' she said, anticipating electric blues eyes and an outrageous grin.

Instead, a man wearing a grim black suit stood at the end of her bed. Dimly, she remembered him from one of the glimpses in the darkness. He looked less like the terror of her childhood dreams.

'How are you feeling?'

'Who are you?' she croaked.

'My name is Detective Rogers.'

She frowned.

'You're the guy that hailed my ship?' She lay back. Holding her head up from the pillow was more of an effort that she'd thought. 'Man, you made him pissed.'

'I'm sorry if he did anything because-'

'No,' she waved her hand. Then despite everything a smile came to her lips. 'It was the first time I'd seen him lose his rag. You really got under his skin.'

The detective smiled at that.

Eleanor sighed.

'So, I suppose you want me to tell you what happened?'

Caleb nodded.

'If it's too painful, the story can wait. Right now, I'd just like to know one thing.'

'What's that?'

Caleb scratched his chin and came and sat beside her on the bed.

'Where the hell is he?'

Day 240

Another night. Another failure.

Smiley returned like a restless ghost to the dim hut in the clearing, skin glistening with sweat and bones aching like a beaten mule. In the months he'd been living out in the woods he'd scoured the forest for miles and miles in every direction and not found anything. He was still sure the writing on the cavern walls couldn't lie. The gate was here somewhere. But he'd begun to doubt himself, his worthiness.

He opened the door and put the gas lamp on the table and then went into the bedroom where he kept what food he'd stored up on the bed. He was ravenous as a coyote.

Food was becoming scarce. The first few weeks he'd lived on cottontail rabbits, waiting in the bushes and then hitting them with stones. There were no rabbits to be found anymore: they'd either gone to ground or he'd simply depleted them. The rabbits had been tender, palatable, good to eat. Now he had to be less fussy. He killed squirrels, bobcats. He currently had three skinned squirrels wrapped up in dock leaves on the bed. He sniffed each one. Two were still good to eat but he had to discard the third. He took it outside and covered it in gas oil and burned it, being sure to watch the flames carefully.

Wild alligator weed kept him from malnutrition. A carpet of the white-headed water-weed grew on the edge of a small lake in the east where he went to drink and fill up Captain Cole's bucket. Sometimes he supplemented it with dandelions and arrow-wood berries but they were few and far between.

Increasingly he was afraid he would not have the means of keeping her alive. He needed her to open the gate. Finding someone else at this stage would be almost impossible: a trip back to civilisation would either cost him his life or get him caught.

He took one of the squirrels and went back into the main room. He slid the table to the other side of the room and then crouched and opened the trapdoor and tossed down the meat. He had almost shut the trapdoor when he realised he had seen something that was not supposed to be there and flung it open again.

Yesterday's meal was already lying in the dirt, wriggling under the attention of worms as though tickled by their mouths.

He remained crouched by the trapdoor for some time staring at the bloody worm's-meat. He knew exactly what it meant but could not accept it. Not now.

Like a sudden rain, the rage fell on him all at once.

He swept every instrument off the table and howled so loud his vocal chords felt as though they dislodged in his throat. He lashed out like a meth-head at everything: the air he breathed, the walls. He tore a chunk of the floorboard up with his bare hands. He took the lit gas lamp and smashed it on the wall and watched the glass explode into molten-coloured fragments. A flame began to lick the ancient, dry wood but soon sputtered out.

That wasn't good enough.

He kicked over the table and then began emptying the spare oil cans until the floor was washed with it; he lit one of his matches. He stopped and stared at the single flame – like a lonely star. He stared into the tiny blue heart of it and wondered what it would feel like to let that burning iris consume his whole body. The fire burned down the match like a fuse until it reached his fingers and he blew it out and remained standing in darkness.

He'd striven so hard to grasp what he saw in his dreams and yet the mystery of them only deepened. Deeper and deeper like a river slowly bleeding into a sea. He was submerged. An artist unfulfilled. The nothingness of the earth pressed around him; it felt as though the four walls of his cabin and the tiny flames within were all that kept that darkness from being absolute. He wondered whether he was wrong and had always been wrong: the darkness meant nothing and there was nothing beyond it and once the intelligence beating within his body snapped out he would become part of the darkness but never cross it, because it had no end. He felt a wriggling pain inside his skull like a breathing cancer; he recognised the pain. He called it by name. It was the sickness of being alive.

It was the sickness of being human.

More potent than even one of his visions manifested the realisation this pain was what he had been fighting to remove his whole life. His eyes burned from looking into too many hollow spaces. Those spaces inside people where souls should be. The book of revelations had come true and the dead walked only to die again. Who was he? Who was anybody? Meat and pain trying to define itself. And hatred. Hatred for all of it. Every second of existence a scream against being. That was his pain, the pain he had to end. Only the gods could end it but what if they weren't real? What if his pain would follow him even into the darkness?

Cole was gone. She might be dead in the woods but given how tough she'd proven he doubted it. She had probably gotten to a ranger on patrol in one of the national parks or even an officer and was describing the way she had come. From there it would not take long for them to find him. They were coming. Fuck. They were coming for him and he hadn't found it. Once he did nothing would matter but he hadn't yet.

He had to prepare for the worst.

He had tools to prepare his ambush: hacksaws, masking tape, a woodcutter's axe, flares, pipes, oil, wire, three drums of ammonium nitrate fuel oil, thread and matches. He could go out again tonight and search for the gate and trap the perimeter. There were still hours of darkness left. What was that cheap slogan his father had used? *Most people give up when they are just short of achieving their goal.*

Maybe this one time his father was right. Maybe this was his test.

Maybe he would fail all the same.

It didn't matter.

He needed someone to replace Cole for the ritual. There was no point running. He was here and so close he now endured maddening dreams where he discovered he slept on the very spot he was trying to find. No. No running. He would lure them in and capture another. Perhaps it would even be Caleb Rogers? Yes, that would be perfect. The thought was so thrilling his heart quickened.

He went into the bedroom and pulled off the bed-sheet. Then he brought it into the main room. He lit another gas lamp and picked up the table and set the tools back onto it. He took the pipes and put them inside the bed-sheet along with a rusted hacksaw, a flare, a drum of fuel oil, wire, and three feet of thread. He went outside.

He got out his tools and laid them out under the stars. First he broke up the hacksaw into little jagged pieces on a rock then pulled off the crusted stopper of the drum and mixed them in with the ammonium nitrate. He put the thread so that six inches of it was dug into the nitrate and then out the nitrate into the pipe and laid the pipe on the ground. He draped the thread in a dry holly bush and then stuck a flare into the ground underneath the bush. He wrapped the wire around the flare's cap and then started crawling backwards keeping the wire taut at roughly ankle length. He attached it to a tree-stump.

When he had finished making the pipe bomb he went back into the hut and scooped up all the broken glass and sprinkled it in a circle around the edges of the clearing as though drawing a summoning circle. He went back to the hut again and grabbed another flare and more wire and then taped the flare to the door frame at around eye-height and attached another wire to the flare's cap and pulled it taught and then attached it to the door-handle.

He grabbed the axe and went to the back of the hut. He hacked at the back-wall until he'd made a hole in the rotten wood that came up to roughly his knee. He put the axe aside, lay down flat on his chest, and then crawled through the opening. It was an easy fit now given how thin he was.

He crawled back in, grabbed a gas lamp, lit it, and crawled back through the hole and then went out into the woods, a certainty filling him up like a sweet smell.

He did not know whether he was being guided or whether his footsteps were accidental but he felt sure he was following a path and not striking out blindly. The gas lamp hung suspended from the iron ring in his hand like the first promethean fire of the world, a fire that had also been a key.

Panting like a dog running over miles to find its master he hung the lamp low, scouring the ground. As always he watched for rangers or other people. So far he had never encountered any.

And then the light of the lamp fell on something glistening and yellow.

He paused for a moment to inspect it. It was a spider, perhaps as large as the palm of his hand. Black save for spots of yellow running down its back, reminding him of a toad.

The spider did not move or flinch from the heat and flare of the lamp. An orange pinprick began to shine in each of its eight eyes. Smiley had the sense that the spider was, in fact, truly looking at *him*.

'Hello, little spider,' he said.

The spider turned and scuttled away into the undergrowth.

Smiley followed it.

Bent like a goblin, he put the iron ring of the lamp between his teeth and went after the arachnid on all fours. After barely fifty yards he reached a small mound surrounded by thick, furry briar. The spider scuttled into it and was lost.

He stood and took the lamp in his hand and held it high so as to see the mound fully. He'd been here before though he'd found it altogether unremarkable. He looked at the patch of undergrowth into which the spider had vanished.

There was something gleaming there.

In the stillness and darkness of the forest, with only the unrelenting stars to see, Smiley reached out a hand to the undergrowth and pulled it aside. The dried leaves were upended easily. He set down the lamp and began digging with two hands. He could not believe what he was seeing. It couldn't be more than 100 yards from the hut where he'd spent months living.

He began to laugh as he tore at the thick leaves. A thorn cut his hand but he didn't stop. He uprooted them all and then reached out and touched the dark oak.

There was a cellar door set into the mound.

He opened it and went inside. A narrow, cylindrical cavern led away. He picked up the lamp and went inside, his senses assault by mustiness and another more acrid smell: a smell that reminded him of sitting behind an embankment and breathing ash clouds.

He followed the narrow tunnel to its end like a frantic rat pursuing the end of a labyrinth. He took each twist without pausing and at last emerged into a small, circular chamber, his lamp throwing a red glow around the room like the shimmering light of Mars.

His eyes widened and tears came to his eyes.

This was the place.

Oh gods, this was the place.

Day 240

Caleb sat in Justin Walker's office along with Michael Delano, Jeffrey Portly, Kyle McGinnis and the Chief himself. On the table was a map of Texas with a red circle drawn west of Houston, nearing the border with Louisiana.

Caleb could not stop his hands from shaking. He withdrew a packet of nicotine gum from his jacket pocket and opened it and put one in his mouth and chewed but it did nothing. He doubted even a cigarette would.

They were closing in on Smiley.

'Before we begin -'

But before Caleb could begin the door to the office burst open and Tom Marvin walked in.

'What the hell are you doing here?' Justin said, standing.

'I've got things to finish,' Tom said.

'You said you wanted out.'

'Consider it my eight weeks notice.'

Justin snorted in a way that reminded Caleb of a bull about to charge.

'You gave me your damn badge.'

'Then hand it me back,' Tom snapped. He turned to Caleb. 'I let you down twice. It won't happen again.'

For the first time in all the years Caleb had worked with Tom he thought he looked different. Maybe it was just his outward appearance that had altered: the black rings around his eyes, the shadow of stubble finally blossoming that Tom had religiously kept in check for nine years, but Tom no longer looked boyish. There was something stern about the way he stood and the way he looked at Caleb. He wasn't asking for another chance, he was demanding it.

Caleb was going to give it to him. Partly because he wanted to, partly because they needed every able body they could, and if there was one thing that could be said about Tom that made up tenfold for his drinking and his lack of attention, it was that he was damn good in a fire-fight.

Justin held up his hands.

'It's your call,' he said, to Caleb. 'You're heading this.'

'He stays,' Caleb said.

Tom went and sat down at the end of the table.

'What do we know?'

'Not enough.' Caleb leant over the table and pointed at the red circle on the map. Caleb couldn't help but think of some savage's map in a dark cave somewhere, the dangerous territories drawn on in bloodstains. *Monsters at the edges of the map,* he thought. The myth had never rung truer to him. They were going to go into the woods and find the thing and kill it. 'He's holed up in some old boy's cabin in the woods about 7 kilometres from the Anahuac National Park.'

'He *was* holed up there,' Justin interjected. 'He may have moved on now he's lost Cole.'

'I don't think that's likely. He's got limited food supplies and nowhere to go. What's more probable is he's waiting for us to come and get him. He was keeping her alive for something, possibly another ritual killing. The only thing he ever said to Cole was about "opening the Black Gate". With her gone, he can't finish his work. It'd be suicide for him to go back to the city to pick someone up so he'll wait for us to come to him.'

'Then we have him,' Justin said. 'Surely?'

Michael Delano was frowning as though trying to solve an equation. 'It doesn't make sense.'

Jeffrey chortled.

'Guy's a whack-job anyway. You expect anything he does to make sense?'

Caleb raised a hand to silence them all.

'It might not be as crazy as you think. Cole said she saw some barrels stockpiled in the cabin along with a whole raft of other hardware. There could be oil or gas in those barrels. Given Smiley was in the infantry there's a high chance he's booby-trapped the place down to the last twig.'

There was a pause.

'Well shit,' Jeffrey said.

'I take it the plan is not to walk right into it?' Michael said.

Caleb grimaced.

'Unfortunately, it is. If all we do is put up a perimeter and slowly tighten it he will slip through. Then we'll be right back where we started. We have a window of opportunity. He is in one location and is not going to run. Risking the trap is dangerous but we've far more chance of catching him out in the open like this than scurrying after him in the dark and having to watch a line 24/7.'

'You'd think,' Jeffrey said. 'But then again we had him out in the open last time. Outnumbered him. Out gunned him. He still got away.' Jeffrey sniffed. 'I ain't ashamed either. Never seen anyone wanted to live so bad as he did.'

'Which is why we'll also set up a perimeter,' Caleb said. 'Cover every base. A small team will go in and raid the hut whilst a larger force will set up a cordon half a mile out. He's tired. He's malnourished. He's no longer in possession of a firearm. We have him. We damn have him.'

Caleb was not aware of tightening his fist and slamming it on the table but after he'd finished speaking he looked down and saw his hand on the table. He looked at it as though it was an item of decoration that was not supposed to be there.

'Caleb's right,' Tom said, quietly. 'There's never been a better chance.'

'And I suppose the reason I'm here is because I am also Acting Custodian of the Armoury,' Kyle said, smiling like a golem.

'We need M20s, flash grenades, everything,' Caleb said. 'No chances.'

'I'll see what I can do.'

Justin stood up.

'Let me get this straight: you want me to sanction a police raid on a premise we know is booby-trapped by a trained soldier? You know the protocol dictates we've got to get Command authority and bomb-squads in.'

'If we lose this opportunity, we may not get another,' Caleb said. 'You put me in charge of this and I want to see it through. I want to put a nail in the coffin of this lunatic forever. I won't make anyone go if they don't want to. That protects APD and it protects you. Volunteers only. Hell, you could even say this meeting never happened and we acted outside of jurisdiction.'

Caleb took a deep breath and felt the calming influence as he exhaled. It was as though a scale he'd never known existed before righted itself inside him. This was bigger than protocol, bigger than Command, this was *everything*. They'd have to put a bullet through his brain to stop him going out to that cabin tomorrow. If he couldn't stop Smiley now then nothing mattered: not his birth or his life or his death.

Justin let out an aggravated sigh.

'We both know I couldn't stop you anyway. Just make sure you fucking get him. I'll speak to some people.'

'Thank you,' Caleb said, and he meant it.

They spent the rest of the night hammering out the details of how they'd approach the location, of what the protocols would be in a hundred different scenarios. Caleb realised that despite how much he thought he knew tomorrow would be equivalent to throwing himself into a dense cloud. He wouldn't know what they would meet until it was inches from his face.

Until it's too late.

More than once he had to push the thought aside. The whole way they'd been weeks and weeks behind him. Could it be possible they'd finally caught up? He dared to hope.

Caleb didn't remember the meeting ending or what words of encouragement he said to the others. Like in a dream he found himself standing outside the APD dragging on a cigarette and looking at the night sky for comfort in the stars like some primitive incarnation of a human. It grew harder to see the stars every year with all the development work. The towers were ever more grotesquely colossal and the number of freight ships, junkers and GCs adding shadows to the sky multiplied and multiplied. Their red and blue safety lights flashed like illusions of the real stars.

'We think we're better than God,' Caleb said. He thought that maybe that was one sin Smiley was not guilty of: he didn't think he was god. He believed he was serving something greater than himself.

'And we'll keep thinking it until we have a fall.'

Caleb turned to see Tom had emerged from the APD. Under the lights of the city and the night sky he looked a little haler – or maybe it was just because he was back.

'I don't know. We're pretty stupid. How many times have we been knocked on the head throughout history? You'd have thought America being young and all that we'd have learned a few lessons.'

Tom laughed.

'I remember this quote from a Roman philosopher we looked at in high school. Fuck knows his name but I think he said: "Happy is the man that can learn from other people's mistakes".'

Caleb puffed again and then cradled the flame of his cigarette in his hands, breathing the dark smoke as though it was balmy incense. He stubbed out the cigarette on the wall of the APD and threw it in a trashcan.

'If I could learn from my own that would be a good start.'

<>ACCESS LOGS</>
   <>MARS CONTAINMENT FACILITY 006</>
   <>RECORD NO. 102014</>
   <>CREATED 08:11:00 27/01/2061 EARTH TIME </>
   <>BEGIN RECORD</>

AS THIS IS GOING to be our last interview I thought I would share a little secret with you.

Why do I think that?

Detective Marvin was rigorously clockwatching. Besides, you have given up trying to find what you are looking for, haven't you? I've told you everything but none of it is what you were looking for. Do you want to know why that is?

It's related to my secret.

The nature of the gods' healing is not fanciful. This is not a fairytale. This is not a vague, indefinite myth. It is specific. People talk about peace through prayer, or meditation in the eastern practices. They are not lying. You know this yourself, don't you, Detective Rogers? I'm sure that thoughts of your human-god gave you comfort when your wife passed.

This peace, however, is fleeting. It is fleeting because it is based on lies: lies of afterlives and promises and stories. They are powerful lies, but lies nonetheless. The peace, the healing that the seven offer, is far greater. It is lasting. It is eternal.

Do you want to know what it is? Do you want to know why I did what I did?

The healing they will bring will fill up the hole that is inside every human being. It is that simple. It is that clear. It is that beautiful. We will no longer horde possessions. We will no longer lust, thirst, or strive to dominate. These are things we do to fill up the emptiness. No. With the emergence of the gods, there will be peace.

Wholeness forever.

<>RECORDED TERMINATES</>

Day 241

The world outside of the humming jeep was silent.

Pine trees stood like flat unreal drawings on a sallow canvas. The colour of the sunrise reminded Caleb of an eye yellow with liver failure: the eyes of his wife just before she'd gone. No one talked. His pistol hung like a talisman inside his jacket pocket.

The interviews went round and round in his head like an endlessly looping tape that was cracking up, fragmenting, running down. He didn't need his monitor to remember them. They had returned like unfriendly faces out of the past and lay down next to him in his bed. When his bladder woke him up in the dead of the night the girl stood at the end of his bed again: accusing him with her snarling scream.

Tom sat spinning the chamber of his revolver. He spun the chamber, sighted down the barrel length and flicked the circular chamber back into place. He then flicked the chamber back out again and repeated the process. His other tick was counting the rounds he had in his pockets.

Michael stroked his thigh as though it was a nervous dog he wished to calm. Jeffrey just sat staring out of the window at the forestry, as though he'd never been out of town.

It was a four hour journey from Austin to the Anahuac refuge where they'd be dropped off and retrace Eleanor Cole's steps as best as possible. Those four hours were both some of the longest and shortest of Caleb's entire life. There were points at which he checked his watch every thirty seconds expecting hours to have gone by and yet at the same time it was only the bat of an eyelid before the jeep slowed and they dismounted.

Tom sniffed the air like a blood hound and surveyed the area. Glistening long-grass stretched for a few kilometres before touching the tree-line.

'Weather's clear,' he said.

He walked around the back of the jeep. Michael Delano had popped the trunk and was handing out supplies: water, handhelds tuned to a secure frequency, two kitbags filled with grenades and mags, three M20s (Tom declined to use an assault rifle), and body armour.

They stood for a few minutes gearing up, punctuating the hovering silence with the clicking of magazines being loaded and the zips on their body armour.

'Let's go,' Caleb said, when they were ready, and the four of them set off across through tall grass like outlaws sent in exile from their homeland into the wild. Soon they were under the canopy of the pines. The smell of the forest was not comforting. More times than he could count, Caleb had gone with Martha to one of the many national parks scattered across the border. Walking in the forest and breathing the unpolluted air had always lifted him. Not now. Now he tasted something in the air that made his skin crawl and his nostrils itch: a heavy, bloody weight in the air that he was loathed to drag into his lungs.

As he clutched the M20 with ever slipperier hands a thought manifested itself like some unpleasant growth: he considered he was going into a place where he was beyond the help of the world of order and cities and numbers. Another planet. Not Mars or Earth, but one altogether more ancient, where the hedonistic and the cannibalistic and the savage still ruled under the open sky without fear of law and order.

Smiley's planet.

All of a sudden he saw a large, unnatural shape and he brought up one hand and flicked it down twice and the others took cover, lying flat in the undergrowth. Michael propped the M20 in the V of a splitting tree and levelled it on the shape. He looked sure and confident. Caleb wished he felt like Michael looked.

The shape was a low, ramshackle cabin, the kind of place owned by an inbred who hated the modern world and everything in it. It was not large and had no windows. Caleb's first thought was that it was a terrible building to have to defend. Someone inside wouldn't be able to see an enemy approaching.

But what if the cabin was a decoy?

It was also possible that Justin had been right and Smiley had fled.

You don't have time to question yourself now.

'What do you reckon?' Tom said, behind him. He had his revolver out. 'The heather gives us some good cover.'

'We need to see if there's a back entrance,' Caleb said.

He reached down and pulled the handheld from his belt.

'Michael, Jeffrey, make your way round to the back.'

He looked over to check they'd understood and Michael nodded at him. He withdrew the M20 from its position and got to his feet, being sure to keep low. Jeffrey followed his lead and they skirted off into the wood.

Caleb and Tom waited.

After a few minutes, his handheld buzzed.

'In position.'

'Anything to see?'

'There's a small hole in the back wall, big enough for a dog to go through maybe.'

'Roger that. Keep an eye out.'

He replaced the handheld on his belt.

'We going in?' Tom said.

Caleb looked at him.

'We have to.'

He crept forward through the undergrowth, careful not to lift his head above the heather. He was fairly sure Smiley no longer had a firearm but he was not prepared to put money on it. He pushed aside a few sharp branches with the barrel of his gun and then fixed it on the door. There was a good twenty feet of practically open ground between the line of trees and heather and the cabin broke only by the odd tree stump or cluster of weeds.

No choice but to make the dash.

Tom's hand suddenly wrenched him back. He stumbled and fell clumsily in the undergrowth cracking twigs and making a loud thump as his gun hit against a trunk.

He got to his feet and rounded on Tom. What the hell was he doing? He would have screamed but knew that would have been a worse blunder than his fall. Tom did not blanch but pointed silently to the ground. Half-submerged in the mud were shards of broken glass, sticking up like the teeth of a buried monster. Caleb had almost stepped in it. He followed the line of the shards and realised they were scattered in a circle around the cabin.

Shit.

He looked into Tom's eyes and mouthed a thank you. Tom pointed to the hut and nodded.

Caleb knew exactly what he meant.

Smiley was here.

Caleb lifted his hand above the heather and made two chopping motions in the direction of the cabin. A hand on the other side of the clearing answered with the same gesture. He took a deep breath which quivered through his body like a lingering musical note then rose like a jaguar to the sight of a fleeing deer and ran across the clearing. He heard Tom behind him. Caleb reached the door in seconds and stood flat against the wall next to it. Tom trained his revolver on the door. They shared a glance and nodded.

Caleb threw open the door. Something like a volcanic light fizzed on the other side and he stared into the light as though hypnotised.

He experienced a strange calm and a knowingness looking into the light: everything was about to spin into chaos, but for that brief second, there was peace and fire and light.

He twisted and threw himself in a dive towards the ground. The flare exploded and fired off a shooting streak of light like some plasmatic cannon. He was quick enough to prevent the flare hitting him in the eyes, its intended target, but not quick enough to stop it pounding into his side like a hard kick and setting his jacket alight. He smacked against the muddy earth and threw aside his rifle. He rolled and patted at the flames.

Two sets of footsteps: one on wooden floorboards and one on the hard earth. He turned and saw Tom sprinting for the door but a moment later there was a second flash of light and Tom went flying through the air. The earth was uprooted and Caleb felt the ground shake beneath him. Shrapnel pattered off his body armour though a few shards sunk into his forearm stinging him like a cloud of wasps.

Tom hit the ground and bounced. When he hit the second time it was like an avalanching stone and he rolled and rolled until he came to a stop by stump. His face was bloody.

Caleb tore off both body armour and jacket and drew his pistol and rose to his feet. He heard gunshots and then another explosion and sprinted around the back of the cabin. His breath caught in his throat. There was a torn piece of earth and an acrid smell like petroleum but more powerful. Jeffrey lay face down in the earth and Michael was sprawled by a tree. Michael was missing a hand.

A shadow was running into the woods beyond them.

'Go!' Michael Delano shouted, deliriously. 'Go!'

Caleb ran past them and after the shadow. His heart had begun to thump like a drum sounded in the dark origins of humanity, a drum that would summon the wargods to arms against an enemy tribe. There was only him and the shadow and everything else was insubstantial.

He fired off a few rounds never slacking his pace. The shadow flinched and stumbled and he knew he'd hit him. He fired again but this time there were too many trees in the way. His breath was sharp and painful. He wished he'd not had so many cigarettes and not drunk so much.

But these things were also irrelevant, because there was only him and the shadow.

He lost sight of Smiley and pushed himself harder, his legs feeling like they had weights attached to them. A moment later he reached an opening in the earth that led down to a tunnel from which ochre light glowed like the glow of a blacksmith's.

He stood on the edge of the opening and then raised his pistol and descended. He entered a narrow, winding tunnel. White roots ran through the tunnel walls and hung from the ceiling like worm-creatures. Flickering orange light drew him like a wisp through the marshes.

After a few steps he felt something brush against his ankle and looked down to see a glistening spider crawling up his shoe; he flicked it away into the shadows.

'And here we are, at last, Detective Rogers.'

The voice. He had almost forgotten the voice. But he wouldn't let it fill up his head with its twisted poetry. Not this time.

'You could have had a career in voiceover,' Caleb said.

Just ahead there was a turn in the tunnel. A shadow played on the wall: a trick of the uneven light?

He rounded the turn, pistol ready, but there was only a further stretch of earthen corridor. He blinked sweat out of his eye.

Soft laughter.

'I didn't take you for a wise-cracker. You really are a man of many talents! I can always admire someone with your determination. Determination is what the gods ask of us all.'

Caleb snorted.

'Is that what you think you have? Determination?'

A sixth sense had emerged in his head that told him Smiley was just around each corner, but whenever he did round one there was nothing there.

'You think I am mad. You know I questioned my own sanity many years ago? Sometimes I still do. But I am not mad, detective. I am merely *enlightened.*'

'Funny how a lot of mad people say that,' Caleb retorted. His hands were beginning to shake and he couldn't hold them still. He felt like he was about to suffocate. There was something at the end of the tunnel now, a room from which the orange light shone. 'Turn yourself over and I might not put a bullet in your brain.'

'You can't kill me, detective Rogers,' the voice said, with mockery edging every syllable. 'I'm inside your head.'

A memory sparked. He'd heard that before, but where?

The prison.

'Is that what you told Rusty?' Caleb snapped.

There was no answer to that final jab. Caleb wondered whether he would ever reach the orange-lit room or whether it would keep growing further and further away from him like a door in a dream.

Something crunched under his foot. He looked down. Bone. A carpet of bones. He went on. The bones flooded from the chamber at the end of the tunnel. Mixed in with the femurs and ribs were animal skulls: deer, cat, dog, lizard and even the odd human skull that looked small enough to be a child's. Nausea swelled inside his chest and he choked.

He stepped into the chamber and stood amidst what could only be described as a dim altar. It was lit by a faltering gas lamp. In places the bones were piled knee-high and blank eyeless sockets stared at him from all directions with accusation only the dead were capable of. Cobwebs traced veils between ceiling and floor, like silver doorways. A spider the size of Caleb's hand crawled over a bleached skull. In the heart of the chamber was a stone table that rose on a thin intricately carved column. At the back of the chamber an arch stood formed out of rough-hewn stone.

A scream.

Just in time he leapt back and avoided the slicing swing of an axe. The blade caught his pistol and sent it flying out his hands. He stumbled on a bone and fell backwards. Smiley was on him again in moments, bringing the axe down in an overhead blow. Caleb rolled to the side and heard the blade thump into the earth with a force that made him think of his own skull splitting open like a cracked egg.

He scrambled to his feet and threw himself forward at Smiley's midriff. He expected resistance but the body he felt under his arms was emaciated and weak. Smiley tripped back and Caleb slammed him against the wall and the axe went tumbling from his hand.

Caleb grabbed Smiley's throat. He stared into his eyes and tightened his grip.

The man he strangled was very different to the one he'd arrested at the petrol station eight years ago. His face was a mess of scars and hardly an inch of skin was visible that wasn't purpled or calloused. A shaggy beard like the hide of a mangy dog hung from his chin and the flesh around his eyes was sunken like a pit.

But the eyes within those pits were still the same: shining, burning, mad.

A knee drove into Caleb's gut. He spluttered but held on. A second one drove all the air out of him and he was forced to let go, heaving. A fist snapped across his face and he tasted blood. Smiley leapt at him, a jackal savaging some wounded prey, howling like a werewolf worshipping a newly swollen moon. Caleb felt teeth bite into his ear and then pull. The lug ripped and flushing pain spread through the whole side of his head. He punched out. His fist connected with something bony. He thrust out again and the pressure lifted from him and he fell back stumbling over bones he was sure were human. His opponent crouched opposite, bloody mouthed and grinning. He spat out a sliver of Caleb's ear.

The axe lay on the floor between them.

Smiley watched him like a panther. Caleb could not restrain his eyes from flicking to the axe to him and back to the axe again. All thought of arresting Smiley had vanished and there was only the thought of putting an end to his life. He knew it was exactly what Smiley expected him to do but all cognitive thought had shut down and he knew to think about what he was doing would be the end of him.

Caleb dived.

Quick as a cat's paw Smiley's booted heel slammed down on Caleb's wrist. A second later the other foot smashed into his face and he felt his nose break beneath the impact and pain bloomed somewhere *behind* his face inside his sinuses. He threw up his hands as the stomping rain began. Smiley hit fast and hard and did not let up, grunting and roaring as he sent each boot cracking into Caleb's ribs, legs, face, stomach.

Caleb felt the bones in his forearms awaken with pain as they struggled to intercept the crushing kicks.

To take much more meant the end of the fight and Caleb couldn't lose now, not when he was so close. He did the only thing he could which was to snap out his own kick. Smiley easily parried it with his hand. Caleb snapped out a second one and this time caught his opponent between the legs and he doubled over and screamed. Caleb rose and smashed an elbow into Smiley's face sending him reeling back. He hit the wall and pushed away from it.

The two collided again clawing, punching. Caleb had been trained at the police academy to box but however hard he punched Smiley threw two back twice as hard, imbued with a strength that came from a rage very few ever came to know. Caleb felt like he was fighting underwater, with the sickly inhibition of a dream. Smiley seemed to grow with each blow he landed, magnifying in stature and terror. His face no longer looked dented and scarred but monstrous.

He threw down Caleb and stood over him in triumph. Both were blood-drenched, Aztec priests about their sacred work. Caleb could hardly move a limb. How could this body ever be repaired? He coughed and blood filled his mouth.

He is too strong, Caleb thought. *Too strong.*

Smiley staggered and picked up the woodcutter's axe.

He grabbed Caleb's throat and dragged him to the stone table and threw him over it like a slab of viscera, butcher's meat to be boxed. Caleb looked at the archway upside down and felt as though he was falling down towards it. He almost imagined he could see something forming in the space between the stone.

'I give you back your purpose,' Smiley muttered. He lifted the axe above his head. Caleb let his hands fall and they brushed against something pointed and hard.

'IN THE NAME OF THE GODS!' Smiley roared.

Caleb's fingers, despite weakness, seized around the object; just as, with a tearing exertion, he flung himself to the side. Smiley's axe cut the air with a sound like atoms quivering. The blade caught Caleb's hand, slicing off all the fingers save his index and thumb.

He screamed. Blackness materialised at the edge of his vision and he felt his core tremble like a planet wavering on its axis from an earthquake. He knew Smiley was already drawing up his axe again. He could not stop now. He drove the object in his good hand as hard as he could into Smiley's chest; it slid between his ribs as easily as a knife blade. Caleb felt it breach the other side, a satisfying squelch of flesh yielding, too easy. Smiley froze, as though touched with paralysing venom. He looked down and saw the jagged antler clutched in Caleb's hand, penetrating him.

'A *horn*,' he whispered.

Caleb collapsed at the base of the table. Blood spurted from the stumps of his fingers and the world spun. Vomit clawed up into his throat. There was so much pain inside of him he didn't understand how he hadn't blacked out.

Smiley fell, slumping across the table. He rolled over onto his back, a child in a field wishing to see the stars. The antler sticking up from his chest was like a bolt sent to transfix him to earth.

Blood ran down from his mouth and spread across the wide circular surface of the table until it reached the edge and dripped, like some demonic fount promising eternal youth. Smiley lifted his head a few inches and looked at Caleb.

A look of triumph spread across his face.

'The Black Gate... is open.'

His head lowered. Something unknotted in his body and then stiffened again, as though at the last instance a gorgon's stare had fallen on him. Breath passed. Silence.

CALEB SAT in the dim light of the chamber and watched the darkness grow and grow. The thing he'd seen forming inside the stone arch became clearer and clearer. It was a human shape. A slender human form materialising out of the nothingness. Christ. Christ Smiley had been right. Caleb felt a panicked cry reach his throat. The shadow towered over him now, dark and featureless in the arch.

Hands on him.

He stared up into Tom's face.

It was marred with cuts and shards of metal still glinted in the skin of his cheek; a Talos resurrected by a smithy god to pull Caleb from the abyss. It was the most beautiful face the detective had ever seen.

'I'm here,' he whispered. Tom looked around. 'What the hell is this place?'

Caleb couldn't answer him because he didn't know.

Tom tore his shirt and wrapped bandages around Caleb's bleeding hand. Caleb looked down and watched the blue cloth turn red. The pain was starting to leave him. He felt incredibly cold.

Before he knew what was happening Tom had scooped him up in his arms. There was a fleeting moment where a low ceiling riddled with white lightning hung overhead and then he emerged into daylight that rubbed his skin warm and air that made his lungs feel light.

'Tom...' he said.

'Don't talk.'

'Tom... You can't carry me all the way to the squad cars.'

'Watch me.'

Caleb tried to laugh but instead decided to breathe.

Tom carried Caleb through the woods as though he held his unborn son in his arms. He wondered whether he and Melinda ever would have had a child and whether he would have made a good father. Caleb began to mutter as though sleep-talking but his eyes were open. Tom picked up the pace.

'The stars...' he groaned. 'The stars...they aren't the same, Tom. They aren't the same...look...' Caleb pointed waveringly up to the sky with his maimed hand. Tom didn't dare look up.

They entered a mist of flashing red and blue lights. Caleb could not hold off the darkness any longer and went limp in Tom's arms.

Tom watched the paramedics load him onto stretcher into the back of an ambulance and kept watching long after the ambulance pulled away. When they were finally out of sight he breathed deep and sighed.

'It's over,' he said.

DAY 242

16TH AUGUST 2068

Caleb woke up and sat up in his bed. He had a headache that made him think his skull was being compressed and his hand felt like it had an iron nail lodged in it. He held up his hand to look at it. An index and a thumb poked out from between thick bandages. He could almost kid himself the other fingers were just curled up out of view. He touched the side of his head and felt a thick plaster over his ear. The entire lobe hadn't been taken off but it might as well have been given how painful it was.

He looked back at his fingers.

The events of the previous night were surprisingly distant to him. An awful struggle somewhere below-ground: in a temple, a dark place. Smiley's look of triumph as the horn went through him. Tom. The darkening stars.

When he looked around the ward he was surprised to see Eleanor Cole sitting next to his bed in a wheelchair wearing a hospital gown and smiling.

'Where the fuck have you been?' he said, grinning.

She grinned back.

'I thought you were Jim when I said that.'

For her sake, he wished he had been.

'Why are you here?'

She held up a monitor screen which showed a bold black headline.

'I thought I'd come and see the hero cop,' she said, teasingly. Caleb rolled his eyes.

'Give me a break.'

She put the monitor aside. She moved closer.

'There was one thing though.' She met his eyes and he knew what she was going to ask before she asked it.

'I got him,' he said. She reached over and squeezed his forearm, as though they were family. She sighed like someone waking up to find their fever broken and the pain had gone. 'He's not coming back.'

'I needed to hear it.'

'I know.'

Eleanor let go of his arm and leant back in her wheelchair.

'What will you do now?'

Caleb shrugged.

'Take a holiday I guess. Justin will kill me if I don't. Always fancied Scotland. See if the whiskey's as good as they say.'

'Fair enough.'

'What about you? Back to the junker business?'

Eleanor shook her head.

'No. I couldn't go back to Mars. Not now. I'll do something else. Plenty of work for pilots that doesn't involve the red planet. Change'll be good.'

Caleb smiled.

'Change is good.'

'Well,' she said, giving him a warm look. 'I should get back to my ward. Could start puking at any moment.'

Caleb laughed.

'Take care, Captain Cole.'

She did a mock salute as she wheeled away.

'Take care Detective Rogers.'

He watched her go for a few moments and then just sat there thinking about everything that'd happened and everything that was going to happen. Then he reached over and picked up the monitor. He sorted through some old folders and found the old interview recordings. He looked at them for a moment, like someone looking at an old car that had to be sold but had been with them a long time, then he pressed delete.

He opened his music library. He only had one song in there and he hadn't listened to it for some time. It was Martha's song. It reminded him of a scene from the years in his life before all the shit: sinking cans, sitting out in the garden, watching Martha hang up the washing, singing that very song.

He slipped the earpiece into his good ear, lay his head back on the pillow and closed his eyes.

As he lay there, something stirred in the coat pocket of his jacket, flung over the back of the chair next to his bed. Yellow and boneless, it crept out of the folds to blink with eight colourless eyes at the world.

It began to make a web.

Epilogue

T he spider bestrides the web-ways. The threads of its making
run to the corners of reality and beyond. The sinews of its
excrement hold together planes of existence, just as an ordinary
web conjoins walls. The strands stretch infinitely, forming intersecting
pathways that glitter and map the cosmic sprawl. Seven points anchor
the web, like the Star of Babalon, a fell sign glyphed in the very fabric of
the multiverse.

The spider departs one of these bright points, following a long
pathway toward another. As light diminishes behind the spider, the
thread enters a populated darkness, alive with forms, like an old wound
infested with maggots. Its eight eyes take in all that exists in and beyond
this abyss. It is dangerous to linger here.

Light, light, light. Moonlight. The pathway ends as abruptly as it
begins, the way dreams suddenly transition from one season to another.
Time moves erratically here. Like a thief of memory it steals moments
and centuries and eons.

The moonlight falls from a pale orb hovering far, far too low in
orbit. Beneath it, the wild landscape of the Seven Lands—named for the
Seven Gods who have left their imprint inextricably upon the geography
of this place—writhes and plummets and rises. The spider, unimpeded

by gravity, follows an ancient thread—invisible to any mortal eye—up toward the filthy and ruinous moon that casts such oppressive rays across reality. Crowning this bloated head is a palace of bone-white stone, a fortress covered in beetle eyes that blinks, staring with a hatred undimmed by the passage of millennia.

Through one of these eyes—windows—the spider deftly navigates. In a wide throne-room of impossible geometries and dimensions it lowers to the floor. Its form collapses. Death takes the spider suddenly. The yellow carapace is shorn the way a caterpillar sloughs off its chrysalid. Shadow emerges, slowly coagulating into the shape of a woman, though a warped one, for she has eight limbs. Whenever one tries to determine whether they are legs or arms, one's powers of observation and discernment are defeated.

Six other shapes emerge from the black recesses of the throne room. Each is a featureless silhouette gifted with but one distinguishing characteristic. One smiles with a Cheshire Cat's white smile, moony and over-toothed. One sports a cyclopean eye that incessantly roves, never-blinking. One wears a crown of seven fell stars.

The Eight-Legged Queen bows to the one bearing the dismal crown.

"The Champion is ready, o King."

Pleasure radiates from the first among equals.

"And what of Smiley?"

"The Fields of the Punished shall serve him well." It is the Mouth that speaks, through a black smile. Many voices gargle in his impossible gorge.

"Then we stand upon the brink of victory," the Horned One exclaims, his phallic appendage—sharp as any katana—seeming to engorge with delight at the prospect.

"There are tales of a new ruler in the City of Lost Souls," the jittery Eye voices. "They could be a threat."

"Let the dead believe themselves kings if they so wish..." This shadow, clad in a nimbus of gold, is hard to look upon. Colours not known outside this reality flash across the room. "...Nekyia long ago rotted. It is more a prison than a world."

"But they say the Mad One has found his way there."

There is a long silence as the Gods contemplate *him*. There have been many realm-walkers, those who have gone beyond the boundaries of their own world, but the Mad One frightens them, for he cannot be controlled.

"I think I will have a use for him, in time," the Masked One says, breaking the silence, though their voice is muffled by the gleaming sea of masks that warp and sink and rise across its face like pelagic creatures writhing in the spume.

"Very well. You may try your hand, when the time is right," the Horned One says. "So long as the Origin-verse remains sealed…"

"It does…" the Eye whispers. "I am forever watching its doors,"

"Then we have nothing to fear," the Star-Crowned King concludes. "Come, let us rejoice, the victory of the Gods is at hand."

READ AN EXTRACT FROM THE
NEXT BOOK IN THE SERIES...

HORSEMEN OF THE APOCALYPSE

THE THIRD BOOK OF THRICE DEAD

CITY OF ILLUSION

CHAPTER 1

The sun poured red over the Circle Mountains like a bleeding wound as they dragged Jim out into the streets of Edge Town. Soon, the sun would dip even further and the skies would melt into purple. That's when Yin commanded it to be done – in the place in between.

Jim was twenty years old and tough, but there were over thirty people in the street: dragging, beating, binding him. Not everyone in Edge Town participated – but no one protested.

They lashed his legs together at the knees with twine rope made from a type of hanging vine – about the only thing that grew on the slopes of the Circle Mountains. Jim writhed like a snake. He shrieked. They tried to shut him up. They hit him – hard. Blood ran from his mouth. A few teeth came loose. But he didn't shut up. Jim didn't want to die. Not like this. As he twisted, he caught sight of his own father and mother amongst the crowd. How could they betray him? Would they really go through with it? But he knew they would. They were afraid.

'Hurry,' someone shouted. A sea of hands reached out and picked Jim up. He was brawny, muscular, but he felt weightless as they lifted him into the air and carried him like a longboat over their heads. One of the townspeople carried a rusted toolbox with a hammer and nails in it. Jim knew where they were carrying him and what they were going to do. He'd just never imagined it would be *him*. No one ever did. He supposed that was how it had worked all these years, why no one had ever thought to stand up to it.

The sun dipped a little further, the red pulled out of the sky as if a giant sucked on the wound, draining blood instead of the venom. Glimmering purple remained in its place.

'Hurry!' the man said again. 'We can't fail again!'

Their efforts doubled and they moved quickly out of the town. There was a small hill only a few hundred metres out on which a withered tree stood. It was the last tree within the Circle, perhaps on all the earth. Its fruit was bitter – like iron.

As they carried him up the hill, Jim caught his mother's eye. They were wide, white like the foam in a madman's mouth. She looked like someone else. But maybe he could break the spell? Didn't she love him?

'Mother!' he cried. 'Mother! Father! Please!'

She said nothing. His father looked away.

They reached the tree. It was gnarled and twisted. Its trunk looked like it was made of worms winding themselves together, turned into an un-living statue. Tiny holes dotted its boughs as if something had burrowed through them.

They threw Jim against the tree and pinned both his hands up above his head. The man with the toolbox scampered forward. He drew out a hammer and nails from his bag. Both were so rusty that brown clumps dotted the metal like fungal growths. *Someone. Anyone. Please.*

They fixed his hands, overlapping, against the rough bark. Jim tried to kick with his legs but several men pinned them to the ground. The man with the toolbox carefully rested the nail against his palm. Jim's skin felt supersensitive – as if tiny hairs pricked up along the inside of his hand. The man lined up his hammer. Jim begged.

'You don't have to do this! Please! Mother! Father! Mother! *Mother!*' But they would do it. They must.

They were afraid.

'Put it through!' someone shouted.

The man drew back the hammer and bludgeoned the nail through Jim's palms.

'Fuck! Fuck you all! Fuck Yin! Fuck this place! Fuck you all!'

The man smacked the nail's head four or five more times so that it sank deep into the tree. Jim shrieked with every strike. Afterwards, the villagers stood back. The sky swirled in a purple blaze over the tree. Crows called. Edge Town was silent. For a moment, nothing moved except the wind. Jim bled and cursed.

Then, as one, they turned and walked down the hill back towards the town. No one wanted to see what happened next, except those who didn't already know. Some of the children fought to stay, but were dragged away by parents who refused eye-contact with Jim. When they got home they looked on from windows and street corners. The older busied themselves.

Minutes passed. Jim pulled at the nail, howling, more to let the town know his rage than out of pain. Blood ran down the insides of his arm, tickling him, warm. His cries washed over the silence of the town. Curses. Entreaties. Promises.

Then, they came.

It seemed like they just appeared –some in the town would believe it. No one really knew the true extent of Yin's power.

There were forty of them – shapes against the desert. They looked different to the inhabitants of Edge Town: a semi-tone away from a tuneful note, not that any music played anymore. But they *were* still human. Somewhere. Their bronzed flesh was a match for the ochre sand that covered almost everything inside the Circle Mountains. Wasp-stripe black tattoos curled around their muscular bodies. Animal bone piercings jangled as they walked. They carried weapons: cudgels and axes made out of human femurs and animal horns. The townspeople called them *Stricken*.

They surrounded Jim - silent. The last light of the sun died behind the mountains. The people watching could barely see what was going on now, but they could hear well enough.

First, the Stricken took chunks out of Jim's thighs. Then his chest.

Then his arms. Then his stomach. He lived a long time. Longer than most. And he bled, more than he could ever have believed was in him. The roots drank up the blood from the red sodden earth. Perhaps this was what kept this tree alive when all the others had died?

When they had stripped Jim to his bones, they ate the flesh and passed shreds of skin and muscle and tendons between them like wine at a feast. Then they cut what was left of him apart. Head. Legs. Arms. Torso. They bagged up the pieces of him and set off.

Soon, the desert and darkness swallowed them.

The sun was gone.

[BUY NOW]

A SPECIAL THANK YOU TO
MY PATRONS

A further and emphatic thank you is due to my patrons, my dear cultists and thralls of the Mind-Vault. The work I do is not possible without their tireless support and generosity. These heroic individuals are:

Ross Thornley, James Sale, Steve Talks Books, Lea Kaywinnet Frye, Jesu Estrada, Tom Harper, Michelle Sale, Christa Wojciechowski, Tia Wojciechowski, Iseult Murphy, Kelly Pearson, E. T. Kennard, & Erik Bergstrom.

Thank you from the bottom of my heart.

About the Author

Joseph Sale is an editor, novelist, and writing coach. His first novel, *The Darkest Touch*, was published by Dark Hall Press in 2014. He currently writes and is published with The Writing Collective. He has authored more than ten novels, including his fantasy epic *The Illuminad*. He grew up in the Lovecraftian seaside town of Bournemouth.

His short fiction has appeared in Tales from the Shadow Booth, edited by Dan Coxon, as well as in Idle Ink, Silver Blade, Fiction Vortex, Nonbinary Review, Edgar Allan Poet and Storgy Magazine. His stories have also appeared in anthologies such as *Lost Voices* (The Writing Collective), *Technological Horror* (Dark Hall Press), *Burnt Fur* (Blood Bound Books*)*, *Exit Earth* (Storgy), and *You Are Not Alone* (Storgy). In 2017 he was nominated for The Guardian's 'Not The Booker' prize.

You can find out more by visiting his website: themindflayer.com

twitter.com/josephwordsmith

patreon.com/themindflayer

Printed in Great Britain
by Amazon

22085823R00128